GEORGIE
ON HIS MIND

GEORGIE
ON HIS MIND

•

Jennifer Shirk

AVALON BOOKS
NEW YORK

Published by Avalon Books, an imprint of
Thomas Bouregy & Co., Inc.,
160 Madison Avenue, New York, NY 10016

Library of Congress Cataloging-in-Publication Data

Shirk, Jennifer.
  Georgie on his mind / Jennifer Shirk.
     p. cm.
  ISBN 978-0-8034-7782-7
  1.   Women college graduates—Fiction.   2.   Brothers and
sisters—Fiction.   3.   Dating (Social customs)—Fiction.
I.   Title.
  PS3619.H593G46 2010
  813'.6—dc22

                                          2010016310

PRINTED IN THE UNITED STATES OF AMERICA
ON ACID-FREE PAPER
BY HADDON CRAFTSMEN, BLOOMSBURG, PENNSYLVANIA

For my husband, who hadn't read a novel in over twenty years—until I wrote one. Thanks for reading, sweetie!

Chapter One

Georgie Mayer's hand formed a tightly balled fist. Little did her brother know he was about five minutes away from a black eye.

She sat up, and her Very Vamp polished nails dug further into her palms as the taxi rounded the corner of her street. Oh, her brother was dead meat all right. Brad was acting like some superhuman rubber shield, bouncing men away faster than if she were nine months pregnant and wearing a Who's My Daddy? T-shirt. He was sly, using those big brother scare tactics in the beginning, but this . . . this was the last straw.

A black eye was probably too good for him. Murder was the only way to end the insanity. It didn't matter that Brad was a cop. She'd either have to murder him or live under his Fascist regime until she died, or worse, until she became like old Miss Wallinger—a spinster whose only joy in life seemed to be painting Victorian birdhouses.

A jury would obviously be on her side.

The taxi came to an abrupt stop outside the condo she

shared with her brother, and after paying the man with her last twenty dollars, Georgie charged up the walkway to confront her date-terminating sibling.

She swung open the door and stood motionless as she surveyed the room. Brad was sitting on the floor in front of the TV, polishing his stupid gun without a care in the world. How perfect. Maybe having a police officer for a brother would finally pay off. Because as soon as he reassembled his gun, took off the safety, loaded it with bullets and instructed her on how to shoot the darn thing, she'd have the murder weapon.

Brad finally looked up when she slammed the door behind her. "Hey, Georgie," he said with a pleased smile, "you're home early. How was your date with Hank the Broom Guy?"

"You mean Hank the *Floor* Guy. He repairs hardwood floors for a living. He doesn't sweep them." Dropping her purse at her feet, she glowered at him. "How could you!"

He had the nerve to flutter his eyes, as if he was doing a bad Scarlett O'Hara impression. "How could I what?"

"You had my date arrested!"

Brad shot up a finger. "Now hold on a minute. I—Hank was actually arrested?" He looked about to laugh, but thought better of it. The first intelligent thing she'd seen him do since she moved back home.

"Oh, come on," he said. "How could I do that? I was off from work all night, just sitting here minding my own business, cleaning my Glock." He held up the barrel of his pistol and gave her an innocent smile. "See? Clean as a whistle."

She snorted. "Give me a break. I know how you operate. You called in a favor, didn't you?"

He dropped his sandy-brown head, suddenly interested in reassembling his gun. "I don't know what you're talking about."

"Oh, you don't?" she mocked, rounding in on him. "Well, allow me to fill you in. Hank and I just about made it to the restaurant—which would have been a record for me—when we were pulled over because one of your police officer buddies said Hank wasn't wearing a seat belt. But he was! And you know what else, Brad? Lo and behold, the officer did a check on his license and found a bench warrant out on him for not paying a traffic ticket. The cop just left his car there, cuffed him, and hauled him to the station. Hank tried to tell him he had a good excuse for missing his court date, but your friend wouldn't listen. It was so embarrassing. Now he has to pay a fine, or they're going to keep him in jail."

Brad shrugged. "Boo-hoo, that's a real shame. The law's the law."

"Admit it. You did this, didn't you?"

He stared at her for a long moment, his lips pressed together as if sealed with Crazy Glue. After what seemed like an eternity, he finally stood. "Okay. Look, all I did was write down his license plate number when he came to pick you up and maybe—*maybe*—call it into the station. In my own defense, I had probable cause for doing that. He had a taillight out."

"A taillight out? You're trying to ruin my life over a taillight being out?"

"Ruin your life? Ha, that's a laugh. You should have majored in drama instead of pharmacy. I'm trying to *save* your life. That guy had no business driving over here to pick you up while there was a warrant out for his arrest. He's the one who didn't pay his ticket. As far as I'm concerned, I just did society a favor too. The mayor may even give me a Good Citizen award."

After a quick prayer for serenity, Georgie flopped down on the couch and covered her eyes with her hands. "I cannot believe this. I wish Mom and Dad were alive, because I would tell on you big time. You're suffocating me. I can't take it anymore." She sat up and shook her finger at him like a windshield wiper on the fritz. "You know you're using your position in law enforcement for nefarious reasons!"

Brad rubbed his hands over his face. "Okay, now listen. You're going to have to de-crank the drama a notch. You're acting borderline *Desperate Housewives*. I just want to make sure you're dating men who are on the level. Jeez, you're my little sister. I have to take care of you. It's what Mom and Dad would have wanted. I was worried about you, Sponge." He stopped for a brief second and, with a pained expression, mumbled, "I love you."

Her lips broke into a half smile. Saying he loved her and using her adolescent nickname took the wind out of her sails. Of course Brad interfered with her life because he loved her. She knew that was the reason deep down inside. And she loved him right back, which made it so much harder to see him wasting all his time still taking care of her. He needed a life.

She deserved a life too.

"You shouldn't be running around with losers like that anyway," he told her, interrupting her thoughts.

"That's the whole point, Brad. *I* should be the one to find out if he's a loser or not, not you. I don't need you interfering with who I want to date or anything I want to do. I'm a big girl"—she threw back her shoulders—"no, I'm a woman now."

Her brother cringed. "A woman?" He grabbed his can of soda and ran it over his forehead, as if he'd just broken into a sweat. "Sheesh, Georgie, you're talking crazy talk. You're not a woman, you're my sister. Did you have anything to drink tonight?"

She shot him a look. "How could I? I never made it to the restaurant, remember?"

"Forgot about that," he said with a smirk. "Well, you're too young to be seeing guys like Hank anyway. What was he, like thirty years old?"

"I'm twenty-four!" Trying to calm herself down, she sat back and waved her wrist with what she hoped looked like an air of feminine sophistication. "Besides, I don't really care about age anyway. Princess Diana was only nineteen years old when she met and married Prince Charles, who was thirty-two."

Brad raised his gaze to the ceiling.

Okay, so he wasn't impressed with her knowledge of May–December romances. That was a bad example anyway since it was a marriage, and it had also ended in divorce. If she wanted to have the upper hand for their next weekly fight over her independence, she'd have to Google a better example.

"Look," he said with a sigh, "get your head out of the clouds and step into the real world. Life's not all about fun and hanging around men who don't pay their traffic tickets. You need to start getting your résumé ready and lining up some job offers."

"No, I don't. As soon as I get my pharmacy license, Al said he would hire me right on the spot." She beamed, dusting her hands together in front of her face for emphasis. "I want to work there, and since I'm already his intern, it'll be a natural transition." Then she could earn some decent money and finally be able to move out on her own. Still, she doubted once that happened her problems with her brother's smothering would be solved. But at least it would be a step in the right direction.

"Yeah, well, I have it under good authority that Al's pharmacy might not be doing as well as you think."

She stared at him, hearing her worst fear come out of his mouth. She needed that job so she could move out. Plus, she loved that store. And she loved the feelings the store evoked in her. While she was growing up, her parents would take her there on Sundays and allow her to pick out any candy treat she wanted, something she'd always looked forward to. Mostly because she didn't have to share the candy with Brad, but also because the decision was always her own. She had treasured that time.

"Wh—what do you mean?" she stammered. "We're fairly busy right now but the summer season hasn't even begun yet. Wait until all the tourists come to town. The store will be a zoo again."

"Hey, I'm only telling you what Walt told me."

She went very still. "Walt?"

"Yeah, Walt Somers. You remember him, don't you?"

She looked away and down at her nails. "Um . . . kind of."

Oh, brother. Walt Somers? The one who was her brother's best friend from grade school? The one who used to live down the street from her family? The same Walt Somers who was, by far, the only proverbial rat she'd ever met in her life?

Yeah. She *kind of* remembered him.

Growing up, Walt always buzzed around their house, teasing her about her braces, mooching snacks, and weaseling invites to dinner by sucking up to her mother. Every time she came home from school, Walt was there. The boy was a menace with a capital M. It was like having another brother—one you weren't required to donate a kidney to if he needed it. This was lucky for him, because she wouldn't have wasted one drop of blood on that pain in the neck.

"Ah, come on," her brother said with a grin. "He was practically family. Hey, remember when he put sesame seeds in your hair and convinced you that you had head lice?"

She gritted her teeth. "Unfortunately." To this day, she still couldn't look at a sesame seed bun in the same way.

"Well, I invited him to stay with us," Brad said, taking a seat on the sofa next to her. "It'll just be for a little while, until he can find his own place."

A chill ran down her spine, and she bolted upright. "What? Until he can find a place of his own? That could take like . . . forever. Why can't he stay in a hotel like every other tourist?"

"Because he's not a tourist and because I invited him. Hey, what's the matter with you? What's wrong with him? He treated Mom and Dad as if they were his own parents, and he always treated you like a sister, didn't he?" A teasing grin broke out on his lips, and he patted her knee. "Think of it this way, while Walt's staying with us you'll have *two* big brothers looking out for you."

She swallowed a scream.

Wonderful. Just what she needed now—another big brother. She might as well get out the phone book and start calling the local convents.

On the other hand, bad news for her could really mean good news for Brad. Maybe having Walt around would encourage Brad to get out more and stop worrying about her. Walt was an adult now too. There was no way he could be the same selfish, childish, thought-he-was-too-good-for-the-rest-of-world type of person. Could he? Well, it didn't matter. If she had to be the adult in this equation, so be it. It would be nice to see Brad relax and have some fun—even at the cost of having someone as annoying as Walt Somers in their home.

With a little luck, Brad might be diverted enough that she'd actually be able to go out on a date in peace and have a little fun herself. Providing she could get another date. She had a feeling her reputation was preceding her.

Georgie looked back at her brother and forced a smile. "You're right, I'm sorry. Walt is like family. He is like the brother I never wanted." He shot her a look, which made her laugh. "I mean *extra* brother I never wanted," she corrected, smiling for real this time.

Brad grinned too, but she could sense he didn't trust her ready compliance. "Yeah, I thought so. Man, I haven't seen him in ages. It'll be cool to have us all together again. Look, you're sure you're okay with it?"

"Oh, yeah. Who couldn't use another big brother? I think it's great that he's staying with us."

Uh-huh. Right.

She was going to hell in a handbasket for that whopper of a lie. The last thing she needed was another big brother hanging around, choking her independence. One brother making her life difficult was plenty, thank you very much. Of course, she'd play the perfect hostess for her brother's sake. Although the more accurate response to Brad's question would've been she didn't mind Walt staying with them as long as Walt stayed far, far away from her.

And her hair.

"Did you run into any traffic?"

Walt Somers removed his sunglasses and tucked them in his pocket, giving his uncle a wide smile. "Nope. None at all. I made sure I left early enough. Philadelphia traffic doesn't start picking up until around seven."

"Oh, good. Are you hungry, then?" his uncle asked, pointing to a table on the porch filled with baked goods and a pitcher of iced tea. "Your aunt Donna made you some of your favorite brownies."

Taking a seat on the chipped rattan rocker, Walt's gaze roamed the quiet surroundings of his uncle's property—from the short expanse of flowering shrubs, all the way to the peach sand and gray-blue waters of the ocean that bordered his backyard. Even on this late cool morning, several people were walking on the beach without a care in the world.

The pace of Maritime City was sure different from Philadelphia, but the change felt right to him. He needed to come back.

"We've missed you," Uncle Al said, pouring each of them some iced tea. "It's about time you took over the store, and I couldn't be happier leaving it in your hands while I'm having surgery. You know your father had always hoped to see you run the pharmacy while he was still living. He didn't think you'd ever return once you landed that big city job with that pharmaceutical company. I have to say, I doubted you'd come back too."

Walt thought about giving up his successful job to take over his father's position in the family business. He was pleased when there was no stab of regret. "Priorities change, Uncle. I didn't like the person I was becoming."

The death of his father had triggered something in Walt. He realized he should have called his dad more, should have visited more. After his parents' divorce all those years ago, his feelings had closed off. He had kept his family—and people in general—at a distance. Maritime City evoked too many memories he'd wanted to avoid. So he had wrapped himself in his work, always having the perfect excuse to remain detached. But when his uncle had called and told him his father had suffered a heart attack and died, it was the catalyst his own heart needed to thaw the defenses he had built around himself. Something had been missing in his life. Walt knew then, too late, that he needed to come home. His aunt and uncle were the only family he had left now, aside from his good friend, Brad.

His uncle made a face. "You didn't like the person you were becoming? You don't look so different to me. You look as you always do," he said, squinting through the thick lenses of his glasses. "A little taller, maybe."

Walt cracked a smile. "On the inside, Uncle Al. I didn't like what I was becoming on the inside. I was so busy trying to keep up with other people and being what they wanted me to be, I lost track of what really matters in my life. Loyalty to my friends and family. That's what's really important."

"And finding a nice girl to settle down with?"

"Uh, well, sure. In due time. Tell me about the pharmacy," he said, desperate to change the subject. Good Lord. He didn't need Aunt Donna overhearing this conversation and calling up all her friends who had single daughters in town. If she did overhear, she'd probably have a date lined up for him by sundown. "Since you're not going to be around, I'm going to need some guidance. What exactly do you want me doing while you're recovering from knee surgery? Do you need me to do more managerial things or work the bench too?"

"Oh." His uncle pushed his dark-framed glasses farther up his nose and blinked. "Yes, a little of both, I'm afraid. I'm short for pharmacist help right now, but I do have quite an intern working for me. She's sharp as a machete. I think you'll like her. She's expecting her license soon, so she's practically running things already. She'll show you what's what."

"Do you mean Georgie Mayer?"

"Why, yes," his uncle said, his grin widening. "Oh, I forgot you were friends with her brother. Yes, Georgie. She'll be your right- and left-hand girl. She's a doll. I know you two will get along swell."

Walt remembered how easy it had been to get little Georgie Mayer all riled up with his teasing when they were younger, and had to chuckle. He was already feeling at home with the memory. "Well, I hope we do get along swell. I'll be staying with her and her brother until I can find a place of my own. No sense staying with you guys and giving Aunt Donna more work to do while you're recovering. It's better I stay out of her way. Brad has been great doing this for me. It's exactly what I missed when I was in the city. Loyal friends."

He reached for his plate but there was a sudden gleam in his uncle's eye, making him draw back and forget the brownie.

"So, you're staying with Brad and Georgie, huh?" Al asked, beaming. "How wonderful. Spending a little extra time with Georgie outside of work might be just what you need now that you're back and looking to settle down."

Walt stared at his uncle until it finally hit him. Mixing business with pleasure with little, chubby Georgie Mayer? Yikes. There was a thought he'd rather not ponder.

Ever.

"Uh, no. I don't think so," he said carefully. "I'm on a bit of a hiatus in the romance department." *True.* "And you know, it's not wise to mix business with pleasure. Besides, I'd like to get settled with the pharmacy and find a place to live first before I venture out in the dating world." *Also true.* "But thanks for the suggestion. I'll give it some thought when I'm ready." *Okay, not true.*

It's not that Walt was a shallow man hung up on looks. He wasn't . . . exactly. It's just that Georgie was practically a sister to him.

His uncle's face crumpled, deepening the creases along his forehead. "That's too bad. Georgie's having a hard time finding a nice young man."

Walt didn't say anything, but he could imagine her having

problems in that area. The poor kid. From what he'd remembered about little Georgie Mayer, she had short, frizzy orange hair, was pale as a ghost, and had braces. A bizarro-world trifecta. He assumed everything but the braces had stayed the same. Nothing against his friend's sister, but those qualities weren't exactly what he fantasized about in a woman. A Muppet maybe.

"You know, Walt, I'll be heading over to the store in a bit, but if you want to go over to Brad's and unpack first and get yourself settled, you—"

"No, that's okay. I don't mind going with you now. I can check things out, scope out the store, and you can introduce me to everyone. I might as well jump in with both feet, right?"

Al smiled. "You're a good man. That would be great. Once you're acquainted with everything, I'm sure I'll feel better leaving you on your own. I really appreciate this, by the way."

"Tell you what, you can show me how much you appreciate it by making a speedy recovery"—then he added with a grin—"partner."

"I like the sound of that," his uncle said with a chuckle. "I'll see what I can do. But I'm sure the store will be in good hands. I have a feeling you have a knack with handling business problems."

Walt nodded. Sure, he was an expert at handling business problems. It was women problems that were an entirely different story. Thank God he didn't have any of those on the horizon.

Chapter Two

"Come on, Georgie," Dee called out. "I've got a doctor on line two who apparently thinks he's above waiting more than three seconds, and Randall's in the bathroom again." There was a short pause. "By the way, this doctor sounds single."

Standing out in the prophylactic aisle of Somers Shore Pharmacy, Georgie held up her index finger to Dee. She needed one more minute to look things over. Something wasn't quite right. And as much as she'd love to start repairing her nonexistent love life, that doctor—single or not—would have to wait.

Her eyes roamed the condom display for a few seconds. Then she saw the problem. Uh-oh. There must have been at least thirty open boxes of condoms on the shelf. And every single one of them was empty. She winced as she scanned the shelves again. The box count seemed higher on second glance.

How could she have let this happen?

She glanced to the right and left of the aisle, and when she was positive no one was around, quietly let out a string of curse words only a woman living with her older brother would have access to.

She felt only mildly better.

Al was going to kill her. All those missing condoms added up to a lot of money. Money—according to her brother—the store couldn't afford to lose now. Al would look to her for an explanation, not his useless employee, Randall. Not that she could blame him. If she were Al, she'd look to her too. Although Randall was technically the pharmacist and the person in charge when Al wasn't there, he was useless when it came to doing anything besides tossing pills in a bottle. Randall would be the last person to notice Fourth of July fireworks breaking out in the middle of the store. No, this was all her fault. She was probably asleep at the switch when some sex-crazed thief waltzed into the store, stuck the condoms in his pockets, and waltzed right out.

Where was her head? Probably up in the clouds like her brother had told her last night. Brad was right. She should care more about her career, not worrying about her social life, especially if she ever wanted to take over as head pharmacist. If she didn't land this job, how was she going to move out on her own? She couldn't imagine working anywhere else. Ever since high school, she'd worked at the Somers Shore store. Her parents had shopped there. Al Somers had made the store a staple in the town's downtown shopping area. She had to come up with an idea to save it.

"Pleeeease, get your bony butt back here," Dee called out again.

Georgie's head whipped back toward the pharmacy department. Dee stood, waving the telephone receiver like a runway flag. Customers were making their way to the counter, and the other phone line began to ring. Randall was still nowhere in sight. What a surprise.

Letting out a sigh, Georgie walked back down the aisle. The condom boxes would have to be cleared away later.

She stepped behind the counter and took the phone from Dee's outstretched hand with a shrug of apology. Holding the phone up to her ear, the physician barked out a prescription order before she could put a pen in her hand, then abruptly ended the call. She hung up and cast a dubious glance toward Dee.

Some single doctor. That guy didn't sound single. He barely sounded human.

Dee finished ringing up a customer and took a cautious step forward. "Uh, sorry about the single doctor thing," she murmured, twisting the end of her long, dark ponytail around her finger. "I didn't mean to get your hopes up, but I kind of got desperate back here."

"It's okay," she said with a shrug, taking a prescription and sitting down in front of the computer. "After yesterday, my hopes are so low I almost tripped on them walking back here."

Dee walked over and laid a sympathetic hand on her shoulder. "Oh listen, honey, I hate to see you so down over this. Last night's dating disaster was a fluke. You've had to put up with a lot from your brother these couple of months, but I think things worked out for the best."

Georgie snorted. "That's easy for you to say. You weren't there. It was like being in my own private episode of *Cops*."

"Hey, I personally like that show."

"It's not funny, Dee. Brad's going psycho on me. He treats me like I'm twelve and hawks over me every waking hour I'm not here." She thought about that statement and wondered if Brad didn't have a patrol car cruising by the place that very minute or maybe even a policeman standing guard.

Standing up on tiptoe, she took a peek out the window.

Whew. No police bodyguard in sight. Okay, so he hadn't gone completely overboard.

Yet.

"He's your darling big brother," Dee reminded her. "Overprotection is what they do best."

Georgie perched herself back on the stool and shook her head. "No. Not to this degree, they don't. Do you know since I've moved back, Brad has not once gone out on a date himself? Once in a while he goes to a poker game at Steve Wilson's house, but that's it. The man has no life, and now he's trying to make me the same way. We're going to end up as the town's only brother and sister spinster team."

"Can a man be considered a spinster?"

She shot her a mock glare. "You know what I mean."

"Okay, I do," Dee said with a laugh. "So you think because Brad has no life, he wants you to have no life?"

She thought about that for a minute. "Well, no, I guess not. I just think he's been playing the role of Mom and Dad for so long he can't stop. Brad doesn't realize I'm an adult now. He needs to stop worrying about me. He needs . . . he needs a diversion."

Dee leaned her chin in her hands and smirked. "A diversion, huh? What are you going to do, order him a stripper for his birthday?"

Georgie mulled that idea over. It wasn't bad, actually, but too temporary a solution to her problem. Plus, his birthday wasn't until winter. She didn't think she'd be able to survive seven more months of the brotherly prison sentence she was in, and she didn't know when she'd have enough money saved to move out on her own. No, what Brad needed was someone else to focus on, someone else to care about for a change. And a little fun.

Dee waved a hand in front of Georgie's face. "Uh, I was

kidding about the stripper," she said with concern. "I didn't realize things were that bad at home."

"They're worse. Brad's giving me a complex. I'm beginning to doubt my ability to make decisions for myself." Georgie picked up a prescription and began entering the information in the computer, then asked, "Is there something wrong with me?"

"Believe me, it's not you. There's absolutely nothing wrong with you. You're just having an off couple of week—er—months. Besides, Hank wasn't so great. You could do much better."

Hadn't her brother said the same exact thing last night?

Georgie finished typing out a prescription and looked up with surprise. "You really think I could do better?"

"Oh, yeah," Dee said, bobbing her head up and down. "Hank had muscle, but no brain. You need to find someone who's more of an intellectual equal. One who pays his traffic tickets would be a bonus too. But someone hot. He has to be hot. Smart and hot. A smart hottie with—"

She held up a hand. "Uh, thanks. I get it now. But honestly, looks don't mean that much to me. At this point, I'd settle for someone with a face."

"A face, huh?" Dee snickered. "Okay, I guess that's a start. But besides the obvious necessities of a body, face, and limbs, what else are you looking for in a husband?"

"Husband!" Her face contorted. "Oh no, Dee, I don't want a husband—unless of course he doesn't want to get married."

Dee stared at her for a moment, her brows scrunched together. "I see," she said slowly. "A husband who doesn't want to get married. Uh-huh, that makes sense." She shook her head. "Honey, I'm sorry, but I'm afraid I'm beginning to see Brad's side of the story now."

She let out a laugh. "I'm serious, Dee. I don't want a husband. Besides, I could never find one as great as yours. And just because I don't want to get married doesn't mean I don't want a man."

After all, she liked men, and she had certain needs like every other woman. She just didn't want the love part. The brotherly love she had from Brad was smothering enough. There was no need to add a husband to that already tight noose.

"Well, then I'm glad I brought this in." Dee pulled out a folded-up section of newspaper from under the counter and held it out to her. "Read it."

Georgie wrinkled her nose, making a brushing gesture with her hands. "Not today. I'm not in the mood for any more dating advice from Ann Landers."

"Just read the headline," Dee huffed. "Clay Hayes is coming to town in a few weeks."

Clay Hayes? Her all-time favorite actor?

"Let me see that." Georgie flew over to Dee and grabbed the paper from her hand. "Holy smokes! He *is* coming to town! He's promoting a TV movie, but he owns a beach house here and wants to give back to the community for all the wonderful vacations he spent here as a child growing up. He loves Maritime City and wants to help preserve the charm that makes the town such a wonderful family resort." She looked back up at Dee and sighed. "That's so sweet. Doesn't that sound genuine?"

Dee chuckled. "Yes. I think he sounds sincere too. And I know how much you adore him. That's why I think you should enter."

"Enter? Enter what?"

"His show, *Until Tomorrow Begins,* is running a charity contest, 'Win a Dream Day with Clay and Rae.'"

"Rae?"

"Oh, you know. Rae Roberts. She plays Clay's love interest, Jessica, on the show. Clay's character thinks Rae's character is little Miss Perfect, but unbeknownst to him, she's hiding a secret so terrible it—"

"*Yes,* I remember now. I watch the show, thank you very much. Get back to the contest information."

"Oh, sorry," Dee said, blushing. "Got carried away. Anyhow, men who enter will win a date with Rae, and the women who enter will win a date with Clay. The money they raise will go to a needy family in town. Clay plans on donating a large amount of his own money for the beaches and to help fix up the downtown area."

"That's nice of him."

Dee frowned. "That's all you have to say? 'That's nice of him'? How about, 'Thank you so much, Dee, for telling me about this. You're the greatest, bestest friend in the world and when I enter this contest, get married, and have his child, we'll name our baby after you and buy you a brand new Cadillac.' "

"So you think I should try to win a date with him, huh?" she asked with a laugh. She shook her head as she folded the newspaper back up. "I don't think so. Sounds like a hoot, but there must be millions of women trying to enter this thing. I mean, what are the actual odds I'd win?"

"One in six thousand—give or take a few thousand."

"Gee, with odds like that, how could I *not* enter?" she smirked. "But even if I did, you're forgetting about my brother. You know how crazy overprotective he's been lately with all the men I've been trying to go out with. He'd actually fanned his gun at the guy I tried to date before Hank."

Dee blinked. "Fanned his gun? I don't even know what that means. Look, Georgie," she said, taking her by the shoulders, "you said Walt Somers was going to be in town. Brad wouldn't dare embarrass himself in front of his friend. Besides, what could he possibly say about Clay Hayes? The man is a complete Boy Scout. Your brother should be thrilled you're finally trying to date someone who's more your caliber."

She raised a brow. "An actor is more my caliber?"

"Well . . . maybe not, but not only is Clay Hayes hot, he's smart. Did you know he'd actually thought about going to medical school?"

"Wow. He did?"

Dee pursed her lips for a second. "Uh, I think so. Anyway," she said, waving away her own doubt, "he has to be ten times better than any of the guys around here, aside from my Brody. You have to do this. Come on, just look at yourself."

Georgie obeyed and looked down, but only noticed a small jelly stain on her lab coat. She licked her fingers and tried to rub it out.

Dee let out an exasperated sigh. "No, no. I mean, look at yourself *in general.* You just said you need to expand your dating horizons. You shouldn't be wasting your time with the slobs in this town. You're gorgeous. Women would kill for hair like yours. You just need to spruce up a bit with some makeup—oh, and lose the lab coat."

Gorgeous? Her? She tentatively ran her hand through her long reddish-blond curls. She didn't know about gorgeous, but she supposed she looked better than average. Better than she had in college. Better than she had in high school. Well, at least better than she had in the womb.

"Georgie, your brother doesn't trust your judgment in relationships with the opposite sex. What does he know? You just said Brad's not doing so hot in the dating department either. And this is a chance of a lifetime. The point is, how do you know you won't win if you don't try? Best of all, if you do win, your brother won't be able to do a darn thing to muck it up without embarrassing himself."

Georgie bit her bottom lip. The crazy idea was suddenly beginning to have some merit. What would be the harm? Well, for one thing, she'd give Brad a heart attack. But on the other hand, he deserved it. She should be able to do whatever she wanted. She didn't need him making decisions for her. She was an independent woman. Sort of. "Let me think about it."

"Well, don't think too long. The deadline is midnight tonight." Dee handed the folded newspaper back to Georgie. "The e-mail address is at the bottom."

Randall finally sauntered back to the pharmacy, carrying an extra large coffee and a pink glazed donut he had to have walked two doors down to buy. Dee and Georgie exchanged annoyed looks.

"Nice of you to rush back for our sakes, Randall," Dee commented, not hiding her sarcasm.

Randall, of course, was oblivious to it. "No problem," he said with a little yawn. "Anyone waiting? I'd like to eat in peace."

"No," Georgie rushed out before Dee told him where he could shove his donut. "We have everything under control. You're free to enjoy yourself at the moment."

With a grunt, Randall sat down and made himself comfortable, as though he was attending his own little personal picnic.

Georgie went back to typing out a refill, but as soon as she typed out two numbers, Dee grabbed her arm. "Hey, don't look now," Dee said in a whispered tone, "but we have an eavesdropper at eleven o'clock."

Her fingers froze over the keyboards. "What?"

"There's a guy over there who's been lingering around the condom section, and he doesn't appear interested in buying any. What do you think about that?"

Georgie carefully peered over her computer monitor and saw a very tall, lean man in jeans and a blue polo shirt. Probably not a local, since he wasn't in the traditional casual garb of shorts and flip-flops. She tilted her head to get a better look, but he had a cell phone up to his ear, partially covering his face. "Maybe he's casing the pharmacy, or maybe he's already pocketed something," she said from the corner of her mouth.

Thinking of the stolen condoms, she started to stand up but Dee's hand on her shoulder kept her on the stool. "Take it easy, Georgie. I didn't say I saw him steal anything. I just thought that he was cute and maybe he was checking you out. Yowsa, take a gander at that body," she said, practically foaming at the mouth. "He doesn't look like a thief to me. In fact . . . he looks a little familiar."

Georgie threw her hands up in the air. "Don't you pay attention to those TV shows you watch? Smart criminals don't try to look like criminals. They try to look like you and me. Besides, I don't care how nice a body he has. I think I should confront him." She cast a side glance at Randall licking frosting off his thumb. "*Someone* has to be the pharmacist around here."

With a chuckle, Dee slapped her on the back. "You go, girl. Show him who's boss."

Georgie gave her a curt nod and stepped from behind the counter. Then tripped and stumbled.

Okay, I can do this, she thought, steadying herself. *Confront the perpetrator. Let him know who's boss.* She was only weeks away from being an actual pharmacist. If she was ever going to prove she could be in charge, she'd have to step up to the plate and show everyone how "adult" she was now.

She slowly made her way up to the man and, taking a deep breath, tapped him on his beefy bicep. When the man swung around and looked at her, she thought her legs would give out from under her—only not from fear.

Oh please, oh please, don't be a condom thief!

Dee was way, way off in her description of this guy. He wasn't just "cute" with his surfer-spiky blond hair and tanned skin. Anyone with a decent pair of eyes would judge a face like his as handsome, almost beautiful—*not* merely cute. But he was saved from looking like a Ken doll by a nose that was slightly crooked and a five o'clock shadow that was already starting to take place at eleven in the morning. In her opinion, it only made him look more approachable and definitely not like a criminal.

She hoped.

The man flashed her a dazzling grin. "Hey there," he said in a husky voice.

She melted under his unwavering gaze and tried to lick her lips, but her tongue felt like a dried-up old sponge. "Uh, hello," she answered, finally finding her voice. "I, um, couldn't help but notice you here, uh, around the condoms."

His grin widened. "Please don't tell me you're here to give me some pharmaceutical advice."

He leaned in closer, and the scent of his pine tree aftershave sent her heart rattling around in her chest like a lottery Pick Six power ball. Gosh, she was pathetic. She was supposed to be taking a bite out of crime, but what she really wanted to do was take a bite out of this man. She snapped herself back to attention and reminded herself why she was talking to him in the first place. Career first, love life second.

She cleared her throat and wiped the stupid grin she felt radiating off her lips. "Um, no. I wanted you to know I know what you're up to," she informed him, trying for a more businesslike tone.

"Well, yeah, I guess I was pretty obvious."

So the man was a shoplifter!

She felt a trickle of disappointment at that realization. What a waste of such a charming specimen of a man. At least he was an honest shoplifter. Maybe there was hope for him yet.

"Well, are you going to show me what's in your pocket?" she asked him.

Mr. Charming–Smells Incredible–Condom Thief blinked, then carefully looked around. "Excuse me?"

She looked around too, hoping he didn't have any accomplices lurking behind. "Look, if you cooperate, I won't call the police."

His cell phone dropped from his hand. "C—call the police? Whoa-ho-hey, honey. If this is your idea of a pick-up line, I think it needs some retooling."

Pick-up line? Huh. Apparently he was already trying to make plans for the stolen condoms. The man's so-called charm was slipping.

"I am not flirting with you," she stressed. "Didn't you hear me? I'm only interested in what you have on you."

He bent down and picked up his phone, looking one part confused and two parts amused. "What I have on me? You mean like money?"

"No, I mean like condoms."

"Wait a minute," he said raising a finger. "Are you still flirting with me?"

She heaved a frustrated sigh. "No. Now just answer the question. Do you or do you not have condoms on you?"

He hesitated, the color in his cheeks flushing a deep pink. "Well . . . I—"

"Ah-ha!" she announced, poking him in his chest. "I knew it. You did steal them." She thrust out her palm. "Hand them over right now."

His already pink face suddenly turned a funny reddish-purple color. "Are you out of your mind? Look, Miss, do you know who you're accusing?"

"I didn't accuse anyone," she shot. "You just admitted it."

"Hey, I didn't admit anything," he shot back. "Not that it's any of your business but I don't have condoms on me." He emptied his pockets before her, pulling out his keys and a wallet, which seemed to contain only a few credit cards and a couple of twenty dollar bills.

She blinked, and her heart began to pound in a frantic rhythm that told her Nice-Smelling Condom Man had just made a very good point. Uh-oh. The fierceness of his assertion—not to mention not a single condom in sight—brought the reality of the situation into focus. More accurately, the significance of what she'd done into focus.

She'd just made a whopper of a boo-boo.

Stunned by her own obtuseness, she looked back at Dee, who—from the tears of laughter running down her face—appeared to have heard and seen the whole exchange. Okay, she may have jumped the gun on this. She'd always been a tad on the impetuous side, a character trait she obviously still had to work on. Worse yet, not only did she fail to catch a thief, but she didn't think this guy would be asking her out on a date any time soon.

Hoping to avoid a store complaint, she tried one more time. "But you were standing here and . . . well, what was I suppose to think?"

"*Think?* How about what any normal person would *think*?"

he asked, his voice rising with every syllable that followed. "You should have thought, hmm, now there's an intelligent, law-abiding customer minding his own business. But *noooo*. Instead I'm automatically marked as a condom thief. Oooh, someone call the cops, there's a man in the condom aisle. I mean, so what? So I'm *standing* in the condom aisle!"

A man clearing his throat behind them made them both flinch. When Georgie dared to look, her boss, Al, stood only a few feet away with his arms crossed and an exasperated expression plastered all over his elderly face.

Wonderful. Not only did she have to answer for the missing condoms, but wrongly accusing a customer too. She was so fired.

Al stepped closer, but surprised her by poking the man in the shoulder and addressing him instead. "Will you please lower your voice and stop yelling about how you're standing in the condom aisle, young man? Maybe that's standard practice in the city, but we country folk just use signs to let the customers know where the products are. And it's no way to speak in front of a lady."

The man's jaw dropped. "But she—"

"No buts. I don't want to be at home recovering from surgery worrying about you and what kind of example you're setting around here. Shame on you, Walt!"

Georgie's eyebrows shot up. Walt?

Uh-oh. Did she hear Al correctly? She studied Nice-Smelling Condom Man's face again with the intensity of an electron microscope, then wanted to smack herself upside the head for not noticing the resemblance sooner. Oh, my gosh. It was Walt Somers. Curse her poor recall ability. Hopefully, he had a bad memory too, and if she made her getaway now, he wouldn't remember what she looked like later on.

Turning on her heel, she stepped in the direction of the pharmacy department.

Al grabbed her by the arm and swung her back around. "Not so fast, Georgie."

She cringed, and Walt dropped his cell phone again. Being the snake that he was, he'd probably make her pay for a new one.

"Georgie?" Walt sputtered.

Walt knew who she was now. Great. She was trapped. Not that she didn't consider making a run for it anyway. But escape was futile. It was fess up time.

"Oh, uh, hi, Walt." Her hand felt clumsy as she lifted it in a small wave. "I guess . . . long time no see?"

Chapter Three

Walt didn't verbally respond to her greeting. He'd have to close his mouth first, and she didn't see any signs of him doing that in this millennia.

"Georgie," Al said, breaking the awkward silence. "Did you honestly think Walt was stealing? Whatever gave you that crazy idea?"

"Uh, well, that's the thing. I didn't know it was Walt. I mean, I do now. You see, he was loitering around . . . and, well, Randall didn't notice . . . then Dee thought . . . and then I thought . . . If I had known . . ." The look on Al's face told her to cease and desist before she hung herself further.

At least she wasn't *that* stupid.

"I can't believe it," Walt said, shaking his head. "I just can't."

Oh brother. Walt was carrying the shocked, indignant gentleman bit a little far for her taste. Although, something in his voice had her looking at him more closely. His surprised expression hadn't changed all that much from a minute ago, but now she couldn't tell if he was surprised because she had accused him of stealing condoms or he was just surprised to see her.

Walt seemed to be doing an intent study of her as well. Then suddenly his thickly lashed eyes crinkled together and a little one-sided grin slipped out, making him look every millimeter the mischievous teenager she'd remembered years ago. Without warning her heart shifted rhythm. Just a little shift, but still, that little shift was disconcerting, especially since she'd known this man before she knew what a training bra was. But she attributed the atria flutter to nerves about getting reprimanded, and assured herself it had nothing to do with the sexy glint in his eyes that told her he'd done quite a bit of growing up himself since the time she'd seen him last.

Al looked past her shoulder. "Dee's waving you back. You must be busy. Once you're caught up, tell Randall I'd like to speak to him in the back room." He slapped Walt on the back and looked at him expectantly. "Well, young man, I guess it was all a simple misunderstanding."

She couldn't resist chiming in. "Yes! That's right. Just a simple misunderstanding. Sorry about the whole mistaking you for a condom thief." With a shrug, she even tried a friendly smile. After all, this was her boss's nephew and her brother's best friend—whom she was unfortunately going to have to live with. For a little while anyway. "No harm done, right, Walt?"

Walt gave her a curt nod. By all body language definitions, she didn't think that was the no-harm-done gesture.

Some people were so touchy. Make one little accusation of prophylactic thievery and you're forever condemned as incompetent. He'd never let her live this down. She could tell that by his facial expression alone. Walt looked at her just like he had when they were young—as though she was still Brad's dorky little sister.

It was just as well. Why had she expected anything different?

The way things have been going for her lately, she'd never be able to convince Walt or her brother she had really changed.

If his uncle weren't staring him down at that moment, Walt would have pinched himself. Hard.

Wow. Little Georgie Mayer had changed.

Although *changed* was really an inadequate verb. He had never seen her look so . . . striking. Striking in a fresh and innocent way—almost as if someone took Little Orphan Annie and crossbred her with Barbie.

Okay, so he was wrong about how Brad's sister would turn out. Who knew?

Sure, the red hair was there, and her face was still on the whiter-shade-of-pale side, but now her skin had more of a peachy-cream sheen to it—something he'd never noticed about a woman before in his life.

Trying to understand what was going haywire with his brain, he stared at the way Georgie's blondish-red ringlets bounced and swayed against her back as she marched back to the pharmacy department. Then it suddenly hit him, like a swift kick in the stomach. Georgie wasn't a little girl anymore. She was a grown woman.

He hated to admit it, but Brad's sister piqued his interest, at least before she'd accused him of stealing. Never in a million years would he have thought the woman he was ogling was Georgie Mayer. He hadn't experienced this kind of immediate attraction in a long time. But now that he knew who she was, he'd have to get his head on straight and treat her like he'd always treated her. After all, she wasn't any ordinary woman. No. She was his best friend's little sister, and there were definite unwritten rules about stuff like that.

Which meant hands off.

"She's something, isn't she?" Al asked, with open pride.

"Yeah, something," he murmured. Really something. He couldn't take his eyes off of her, even when she stopped to talk with a customer. He still had a hard time trying to mesh in his mind the woman before him and the girl he had known.

His uncle chuckled. "Georgie's a spitfire and a little rash, I admit, but she means well. She'll be a great asset here once she gets her dispensing license."

"As long as she doesn't accuse any more customers of stealing and drive them all away before that happens," Walt said wryly.

"Nonsense," his uncle said with a wave of his hand. "She made a small blunder. Don't hold that against her. The pharmacy is doing just fine."

He pulled himself back down to earth and gave his uncle a sharp look. "Is the pharmacy doing fine?"

"We're doing as well as can be for right now. Don't you worry, though. Once summer hits, we'll be hopping again."

Walt didn't comment further, although he suspected the pharmacy was slowly losing money to the bigger corporate-owned stores popping up in the area. Walt hoped his uncle was right about business picking up in the summer. He'd have to use his financial expertise and take a closer look at the books to see exactly where they stood.

"I hope you can get past this little mishap with Georgie," Al said. "I need you to continue training her while I'm re-covering. She's still technically a student. Maybe show her some of those business skills you've acquired in the big city. She could use some more mentoring."

Walt couldn't argue with that. Georgie just proved she could use advice in the business department.

His gaze sought her out again. He noticed that she'd gotten her lab coat caught on the endcap of the aisle and was in the midst of a tug-of-war with the metal shelving. He didn't want to be amused, but his lips twitched at the sight. At least he found it reassuring to see the old Georgie somewhere in that beautiful woman's body. Then he kicked himself for noticing she was a woman again. And that she had a beautiful body.

He cleared his throat. "I'll see what I can do," he told Al. "I'm sure I could teach her a thing or two. After all, Georgie is practically like a sister to me." *Yeah, you just keep reminding yourself that.*

Al gave him an approving grin. "That's very kind of you. See? Readjusting to small-town life is like riding a bike. Even an ex-city pharmacy supervisor like yourself won't have any problems here at all."

Walt's gaze shot back to Georgie just as she flipped one of her long springy ringlets from her shoulder, and he sighed. Never before had he been so mesmerized by a head of hair. He couldn't help but wonder what it would feel like to bury his hands in that massive mane of strawberry-red curls and another unexpected shot of desire coursed through him.

Not quite the "brotherly" reaction he wanted to have at the moment.

No problems? He rubbed the back of his neck and hoped his uncle was correct in that aspect. But something about working and living with his best friend's sister had him thinking his problems may have just begun.

"That went well."

Georgie glared at Dee as she stepped behind the counter. "Oh, stuff it."

Dee laughed. "I told you he didn't look like a thief," she said in a sing-song voice.

She raised a hand to her forehead and hung her head. "I know! I know you did. Why didn't you stop me?"

"To be honest, I thought it was a good opportunity for you to meet a man. A little unorthodox maybe, but I figured since you're going to enter that dream date contest, anything went at this point."

Georgie's head sprang back up. "I didn't say I was going to enter that contest. I said I'd *think* about entering that contest. And I've now just decided that I won't. How can I even consider something like that? I just accused the owner's nephew of stealing! Ugh. I wanted so much to prove I could really take charge, but all I proved was how big of an idiot I am."

Dee raised her fingers to her lips, but it didn't hide the sound of her chuckle. "There, there, honey. It took real nerve to do what you did. Al wasn't mad at all."

"Yeah, but Walt's another story. How am I ever going to face him again? And he's going to be living under the same roof with me. What if he tells Brad? There'll be no living that down. How mortifying."

"Yeah. Walt did seem pretty upset. His face turned a color unknown even to Crayola."

Georgie shot her a withering glare. "Just so you know, that comment isn't making me feel better."

"Oh. Sorry. Well, look on the bright side. He does look good, doesn't he?"

Unfortunately, yes. Walt Somers did look good. She squinted into the aisle where Walt was still talking with Al, to make sure she hadn't been seeing things.

She hadn't been seeing things.

Walt looked very good. But she dismissed such thinking as more of the temporary insanity she'd already been experiencing today. Walt was still . . . Walt. And he was still as overbearing as her brother.

"I wouldn't be complaining if my brother's friend looked

like that," Dee added, as though she'd read her thoughts. "He's still single, isn't he?"

"How am I supposed to know? I couldn't care less." Georgie marched over and, with a pasted-on smile, took a prescription bottle from a customer's hand and typed the re- fill number in the computer. "This will be ready in a few minutes, Mrs. Barkat," she told the older woman.

See? It's obvious. Business as usual. I'm not interested in Walt. But for some reason she couldn't resist peering back down the aisle to see what he was up to.

Dee grabbed Georgie's wrist and pulled her away from the counter. "What do you mean, you couldn't care less?" Dee asked, lowering her voice. "You were just giving me a tearful Sally Fields speech about how you have no life and can't get a date. God answered your prayers and delivered you tall, blond, and hunky."

"Don't be so blinded by appearances," she whispered back. "Besides, I know Walt. He's a weasel. I'm sorry, but bossy pain-in-the-necks are not my type."

Dee snorted as she took the label from the printer. "I don't understand what your problem is with Walt."

"I don't have any problem. Just because he's Brad's friend doesn't mean he has to be mine. I saw how much my parents doted on Walt. He milked every second of it. It was disgusting. Besides, there was the same she's-just- a-kid attitude in his eyes when he looked at me just then. Trust me, it wouldn't work. We're as opposite as . . . as that political commentary team Mary Matalin and James Carville."

Dee's face fell. "Uh, Georgie, they've been married for over ten years now."

They have? "Oh. Well, you know what I mean," she said

irritably, picking up and shoving a bottle of penicillin in Dee's hands.

Dee shrugged and poured some tablets onto the counting tray. "Okay, okay. Fine. All I'm saying is maybe Walt isn't the same person he was when he was teenager. Give him a break. People do change."

At that moment, Georgie looked up and saw Walt swaggering toward them. Ignoring the triple flip her heart performed, she walked over to the counter. Her response to him was borderline ridiculous. Walt may have filled out physically—in very attractive ways—but he still bore the same old know-it-all attitude of the past. "My judgment stands until further notice," she murmured to Dee, then braced herself for Walt's teasing assault.

When Walt reached her, however, he surprised her by extending his hand in a friendly, nonderisive way. "I was thinking, Georgie, you're right. No harm done. I guess I did look kind of suspicious back there."

She stared down at his hand. His reaction was a twist to what she'd expected. She hesitated a moment longer, still not sure what to think of his change in attitude, but then put her hand in his. Walt had a solid yet surprisingly gentle grip, which felt very much like putting on a favorite pair of warm mittens.

Warm mittens that gave you a tingly feeling throughout your entire body.

She snatched her hand back and tucked it under her arm. "Yeah, you did act suspicious. But I think it was your beady eyes that pushed me over the edge."

Walt chuckled. "Look, I'm sorry about how I reacted back there. You threw me off guard. I wanted you to know that it's no big deal. Let's put it behind us."

She frowned, giving him a sideways glance. This didn't

sound like the Walt she'd remembered. If she didn't know better, he sounded almost . . . nice and respectful. What was he trying to pull? Maybe she was being overly analytical, but she couldn't help it. After all, she was a science major.

"Thank you," she said, still not trusting him. "I'm glad you're not mad. But are you going to tell Brad about this?"

"Hmm, well, that's an interesting question," he said with a mischievous smile. "I'm still on the fence. But don't worry; I'm sure you'll get a favorable outcome with a little persuasion. Like maybe . . . breakfast in bed tomorrow?"

Now *that* sounded like the Walt she'd remembered!

"Nothing fancy," he blurted when he saw her scowl. "Bacon, some scrambled eggs, fresh orange juice, oh, and rye toast, but only if you have it. No need to make a special trip to the store just for me." He casually leaned his elbow on the counter and treated her to a charming grin.

She felt a smile threatening, but nipped it in the bud before he could see it. "You know you're a rat, don't you?"

Walt frowned, but the laughter still showed in his eyes. "Hey, now that's not the way to sway my decision in your favor."

"I'd love to hear more of this tantalizing extortion negotiation," Dee interrupted, walking over and waving a piece of paper in her hand, "but Randall's in the can again, and I can't read what drug this is."

"It says Biaxin five hundred milligrams." Georgie looked back up at Walt and gestured to her friend with her thumb. "Do you remember Dee? She's now our full-time technician and all around resident smart mouth."

"Yeah, I remember you," he said, studying her face. "Except for the smart mouth part. That should make things interesting while I'm working here."

Georgie felt the blood drain from her face. "Huh? What do you mean, you'll be working here?'

Walt shot her a challenging look. "Just what I said. Al and I have become partners."

"Partners? Al never mentioned this to me. You mean we're going to be living and working together?"

"Don't sound so thrilled. But yes, I didn't want to be any more of a burden to my aunt while she's taking care of Al, and I had to forget about renting a place. With the summer almost here, everything is practically booked up. Brad was cool enough to offer me your place until I can find a place of my own to buy."

"Oh, yeah, that's Brad all right," she murmured. "Mr. Benevolent." *Except toward his own sister.*

Dee fanned her face with the prescription and smirked. "Well, isn't this going to be cozy? It's like right out of *Bosom Buddies.*"

With an amused look, Walt scratched his head. "Uh, yeah, except for the dressing like a woman part. Unless Brad's into something I don't know about."

Dee laughed, and Georgie sighed.

"Hey, don't look so grim, Georgie," he said, giving her a few pats on the hand. "We're practically like family. I promise to be on my best behavior the entire time. No head lice jokes. Don't want you getting sick of me before I can find my own place, right?"

Yeah, well, too late. She was already sick of him.

"Oh, and your Nancy Drew routine was pretty darn cute back there, I admit," he added, "but next time leave the cops and robbers playing to your brother. Accusing your customers of stealing isn't good store policy."

She planted a fist on her hip. "You were snooping around the aisle. It was a logical assumption."

"Ah, but you never gave me a chance to explain. The reason I was snooping was because I saw a lot of opened and empty boxes of condoms on the shelf. I assume you realize the store was robbed?"

Her anger deflated. She wondered if Al noticed the stolen condoms too. "Yes, I noticed the empty boxes. That's why I thought you were the thief."

"And returning to the scene of the crime? Not a very bright thief, I might add." His smile blazed out at her, and she noticed how white his teeth were against his tanned skin. It made his smile all the more attractive. Almost too attractive for his own good.

"Well, I didn't have time to run an IQ test by you," she said wryly. "I had to go by your dim-witted appearance alone."

"Cute. But I think it might be a good idea to keep this from Al until after he's back from his surgery. No sense having him worry. I don't want anything interfering with his recovery. It might even be a matter of time before the store gets hit for something bigger than just condoms. I'd like to go over the books as soon as possible and check things out to make sure we haven't lost money elsewhere."

She remembered what Brad had said the other day about the pharmacy losing money and became concerned. "Do you think there's a problem?"

"I'm not sure. Once I take a look at all the numbers, I can make a fair assessment. Then I'll decide what to do."

"Well, since I'll be a pharmacist here soon, I hope you plan on including me in what you find and what you plan to do."

"Look, Georgie," he said with a sigh. "You don't need to worry yourself about stuff like this. Just do your job, sit tight, and don't do any more rash things."

His attitude was so condescending she became indignant.

"Sit tight? That response is so typical of someone like you. For your information, I'm very capable of handling these things. I'm not someone who needs sheltering. Anyone who thinks that is just . . . just . . ."

His eyes narrowed and he leaned in close, so close she could see that his eyes weren't simply light brown like she'd first thought. They had a fascinating mixture of green and gold in them, which at the moment flashed at her like hot lava.

"Anyone who thinks that is just what, exactly?" he asked. "At least I have enough sense not to try to pick up a possible sex-starved stranger in the condom aisle."

"I wasn't trying to pick you up! I told you that." *And stop trying to distract me!*

"Could have fooled me. And you were doing a lousy job of it, by the way. No wonder you're having men problems."

She sucked in her breath as if she'd been kicked in the stomach. "Oh. My. Gosh. I can't believe you just said that. Who told you I was having men problems? I am not having men problems. Hey, Dee," she called over her shoulder, desperate for some restoration to her bruised ego. "Am I having men problems?"

Dee paused in her typing and looked up. "She's having men problems," she said flatly, then went back to typing.

Walt laughed out loud.

"Traitor," she muttered. "I'll remember that when I get my license and become your boss."

"Just remember this," Dee said, whipping out the newspaper article on the Clay Hayes contest again, "and who gave it to you when you finally meet your Mr. Dreamboat."

Walt's attention perked up and his eyes shot to Dee. Leaning over the counter, he snatched the newspaper from her hands. "What's this about Mr. Dreamboat?" he asked with a curious grin.

Georgie made a grab for the paper, but Walt was quicker and held it just out of her reach. As he unfolded the article, his brows narrowed as his eyes shifted over the words for several long seconds. When he finished, he crumpled the paper and tossed it in the trashcan behind her. "Wow," he said with a scowl, "I can't believe women fall for stupid contests like that."

"Hey!" She lunged for the ball of paper and pulled it out of the garbage. "I resent that. That contest isn't stupid," she said, unraveling and smoothing the article out on the counter. "I was thinking of entering."

"That's my girl," Dee cheered.

Walt gave a short laugh. "I'd think again if I were you."

Georgie stopped fiddling with the newspaper and looked up. "Why would I need to think again? Clay Hayes is a handsome television star, and I could spend a day with him. He's smart and charming too—something you obviously have no clue about. Sounds like the perfect date to me. And since Brad has pretty much eliminated any eligible dating man within a thirty-mile radius, I'd say it's the perfect solution to my so-called man problem."

"Oh, come on. Brad is not going to let you enter that contest. For one thing . . ." He looked to Dee for help, but she turned away, feigning more interest in filing the stack of prescriptions. "All right . . . for one thing," he said, turning back, "you're too young."

He might as well have said she was too ugly or too skinny, because it ticked her off just the same. "I'm twenty-four. That's only seven years younger than you and Brad."

"Well, what makes you think you could win this contest anyway?" He tapped his index finger down so hard on the article she thought he was going to smear Clay Hayes' poor face. She tried sliding it away from him, but he braced his other hand on the article and held tight.

"Shows how much you know," she countered, still trying to pry his hands away from the newspaper. "I have as good a chance as anyone else. Clay Hayes loves this town. He's probably here a lot when he's not working. When I win, I'll give him my own personal tour."

Walt's mouth hung open. "Well, if you win—and that's a big if—you're going to draw a lot of attention. Do you want that? There'll probably be a bunch of publicity involved and reporters and people hanging around, not to mention—" Walt stopped himself short and hung back slightly. A funny expression crossed his face—not a pleased look but not a totally unhappy one either, almost as if he was hearing Polka music play in his head.

"Not to mention what?" she asked, forgetting their tug-of-war with the newspaper.

Walt opened his mouth again but closed it when Al came up and placed a hand on his shoulder. "Come on, Walt. Randall's in the stockroom. I want to introduce you two and go over your schedules. You and Georgie will have plenty of time to catch up later."

Walt nodded, but he still had a dazed look on his face. "Sure, Uncle Al. Be right there."

Al smiled, giving Georgie a quick wink, then walked away. Walt watched him go, keeping his eyes trained on his uncle's back. His eyes narrowed slightly, and from the way the vein in his left temple became visible, she was sure his brain was about to explode at any second.

"Not to mention what?" she asked again when Al had disappeared into the storeroom.

He whipped his head back to look at her and blinked. "Uh, nothing. Just don't enter that thing," he said, tapping down on the article for emphasis. The pointed look he gave told her there was nothing left to discuss. As if he didn't trust her, he swept the crumpled up newspaper off the counter and shoved it under his arm, then stormed away.

Annoyed that Walt would pull the big brother routine on her only twenty minutes into their reunion, Georgie planted a hand on her hip. "Did you hear that, Dee?"

"Yep. Heard it and saw it."

"See? He's just as bad as Brad. No, worse. I didn't think something like that was possible. Who is he to tell me not to enter?"

Dee cocked her head, not hiding her amusement. "Ah, yes, spite. Always a good reason to enter a contest."

Georgie looked at her with surprise. "Oh, no. I'm not entering myself, Dee. I just said that stuff back there because Walt irked me. No, I'm going to enter Brad in that contest. I think it'll be good for him if he could win a date with Rae Roberts."

"Brad? You're going to enter *Brad?* Honey, are you sure that's a good idea?"

"Positive. This is just the kind of diversion my brother needs. He has to stop worrying about my love life and start concentrating on his own. If he wins, that could really loosen him up and get him back into the dating swing again."

"Uh, maybe you should reconsider the stripper option."

She laughed. "No, Dee. No stripper. He needs a real date."

In fact, Brad needed a long-term distraction; if she were lucky he might even enter into a relationship with the woman. That would really take his mind off mothering her—or *brothering* her as the case may be—and she could get her own life back.

"Okay," Dee said. "But are you absolutely sure you want to do this for Brad and not just because Walt thinks it's a stupid contest?"

She waved her friend's question away and began pacing the floor. "Yes, yes, of course. What kind of person would that make me out to be?" Petty? Selfish? No, she was considerate. She was a caring, considerate sister. In fact, she's sure she would've thought about entering Brad in the contest even if Walt hadn't made such a stink about it.

Pretty sure, anyway.

But she only had until midnight to enter him. Would she be able to find yesterday's newspaper and get the information in time? Maybe she could cause some sort of diversion and grab the newspaper article from Walt, get the e-mail address, and slip it back before he noticed anything amiss. Yeah, that sounded good. But that job was going to require some tricky maneuvering on her part.

"Well, I'm glad you're sure." Dee stood and pulled out a slip of paper from her lab coat pocket. A droll grin curved her lips as she held the paper out between her first two fingers. "Because I copied down the e-mail address right here just in case you chickened out."

Georgie let out a laugh. Who needed tricky maneuvers when you had tricky friends?

"Oh, Dee," she said, hugging her friend, "remind me never to underestimate your sly talents."

"Don't you worry. I won't. But if Brad wins and suddenly decides to declare jihad on anyone involved in this scheme, you didn't get that e-mail address from me."

"Agreed." Georgie glanced down at the piece of paper in her hands and grinned. Brad was going to be so surprised. He could finally relax and have fun, without worrying about her for a change. Then she could do what she wanted, when she wanted, and with whom she wanted. Life was about to get good.

Unless Brad didn't win. Then she'd be back to square one, and they'd both be back to living like hermits. For her sanity's sake, she'd have to come up with a plan B.

Luckily, thanks to Walt, she already had an idea.

Chapter Four

Walt hoped it looked as if he were enjoying a leisurely night of watching *Ultimate Fighting Championship* on TV—because he was far from feeling enjoyment. It was just as well, though. Two-time champion Kent Franklin was getting rocked, and Brad's old sofa was crippling his back. No wonder he felt edgy and restless and unable to think about anything but his friend's sister.

Maybe he shouldn't have been so hard on Georgie, ordering her not to enter that date contest today. What was it to him? He didn't really care one way or another what she did. It was her life. She was obviously a grown woman. For one brief moment, he even considered it to be a good publicity stunt for the pharmacy too. So why had he acted so over-bearingly?

Because something had overtaken him. Something he couldn't quite describe.

A protective instinct? Yeah, yeah, that's what it was—a protective instinct. A *brotherly* protective instinct. It wasn't jealousy he'd felt toward that actor Clay Hayes. He was just looking out for his little "sister" and worried about her getting tangled up with some celebrity hot shot. Georgie and Brad were the closest things to siblings he had. It was only natural he'd want to look out for her.

Walt carefully let out a relieved breath so as not to draw any undue attention from Brad, who was sitting next to him. He felt better already, because now he knew his actions today had everything to do with loyalty to his friend and absolutely nothing whatsoever to do with how beautiful Georgie had become. Or anything to do with those gorgeous baby-blue eyes of hers. Or the way her lab coat seductively clung to her body. Or . . .

Oh, crap.

"So, who's the lucky woman?"

Walt choked and spit out his beer at Brad's question. "What? Huh? I'm not thinking about any woman." He averted his eyes and brushed down the front of his shirt, making sure to block out any lingering thoughts he had about Georgie.

Brad placed his own beer down and frowned. "Easy, man. I wasn't offering a penny for your thoughts. You seem a little out of it, so I figured there had to be a woman involved somewhere."

"Uh, no, there's no woman. Not that my uncle hasn't hinted that there should be one. But you're one to talk. What about *you*? If you're sitting here with me, eating mediocre pizza and drinking lukewarm beer, I'm gonna guess your love life isn't so hot either."

Brad shrugged and turned his attention back to the TV. Walt reached for another slice of pizza, grateful Brad had decided not to pepper him with any more questions. Women were not a topic Walt cared to discuss at the moment. When he was good and ready he'd look for a nice local girl who sparked his interest. He didn't have time for that now. He still needed to begin planting his life here in town. He needed to find a place to live, meet some more people, get the business situated. Adding a woman to that mix would only cause complications.

"So, have you seen Georgie yet?" Brad asked.

Walt's heart did a short tap dance—not quite a Fred Astaire rendition, but a tap dance nonetheless—at the mere mention of her name. Uh-oh. Not good. And not a simple complication, but a major complication, which was exactly why Georgie wasn't a topic he wanted to delve into either.

Walt took a few more slugs of beer, hoping it would snap some sense into him. "Uh, yeah, I saw her. We . . . we barely recognized one another." True, but a minor understatement.

Brad scratched his chin. "Yeah, I guess it has been a while. Man, I'm glad you're here now. Maybe you can take some of the heat off of me. Georgie and I can't seem to do anything but argue since she's come home from college."

Although Walt didn't want to be reminded of Georgie since it only led to thoughts he shouldn't feel comfortable with, he couldn't resist prying out information about her. Good grief. He wanted to smack himself. Back in his hometown less than a day and he was already thirty-one going on thirteen. "Oh, yeah? What kind of problems could you be having with Georgie?"

"You know," Brad said, looking hesitant. "I guess the usual brother-and-sister type stuff."

"No, I don't know. If I'm going to have to start acting as referee between you two, you might as well enlighten me now."

Brad's gaze flicked to his, then he quickly looked away again. "Well, for one thing, she thinks"—he cleared his throat, then gave a weak laugh—"now get this, she thinks that I butt into her life too much."

Walt didn't have any siblings to fully understand Brad's problem, but fights over independence didn't seem so out of the ordinary. He supposed it would only be natural for Georgie to feel the pressure of living with a big brother police officer. "All right, I guess I can see where this could be an area of tension between you two. But, uh, between you and me . . . do you butt into her life?"

"Well, of course, I do!" Brad shot to his feet and started pacing the room. "I'm her brother. She doesn't have anyone but *me* to butt into her life. Sheesh. But she acts as though it were a federal crime. Believe me, it's not. I should know."

Walt shot up his hands in surrender. "Whoa, take it easy. I was just asking."

"Huh? Oh." Brad sighed, slowly rubbing his face and then pressing his fingers into his eye sockets. "Sorry. I think looking out for Georgie is making me a little crazy. I don't know what goes on in her brain sometimes. She doesn't always make the best decisions for herself."

Walt let that comment slide. He saw for himself Georgie's less than perfect decision-making process this morning at the pharmacy, but decided not to share that information with Brad. Good Lord. All he needed was to get a man who was licensed and trained to shoot a firearm more upset than he already was.

"I mean, you should have seen some of the characters she had lined up to go out with," Brad said, frowning down at him. "Do you remember Tim Clark from swim club?"

Walt crushed the beer can he had in his hand.

She wanted to go out with Tim Clark?

In ninth grade, Tim had gotten two days' suspension for sneaking into the girls' locker room and hiding out in the showers. He wasn't the brightest bulb on the Christmas tree, and perhaps a little too curious as a preteen too. What was she thinking? A girl like Georgie shouldn't be dating a character like that.

Brad pointed to the mutilated can Walt still had clutched in his fist. "My sentiments exactly. Which is why I need you to do me a favor."

Walt had a sudden pleasant mental picture of showing up at Tim Clark's home and making certain the guy would never bother Georgie again, so he nodded without hesitation. "Sure. Anything you want."

"Great," Brad said, flopping down on the sofa next to him. "Because I'd like you to keep an eye on Georgie for me."

Keep an eye on Georgie?

Walt nearly fell over. The beer he'd just finished must have already gone to his head, so he reached for his pizza again and shoved half of it in his mouth, thinking he needed more food to combat the effects of the alcohol. He couldn't have heard Brad right. What Brad had probably said was, "I'd like you to dye Georgie's hair for me." Yeah. That's what he must have said. That made more sense.

Okay, not really. But compared to the latter, it was starting to sound like a much more attractive alternative.

"I'm sorry," he said, choking down the pizza and returning his attention to Brad, "I must not have heard you right. What did you say?"

"I said I'd like you to keep an eye on Georgie for me."

He *had* heard right. Why did he have to be such a loyal friend? Now he could have kicked himself for being so readily agreeable to Brad's requests. Threatening and possibly causing some bodily harm to a potential boyfriend of his friend's sister was one thing, but this . . . spying on her business was too much to ask. Especially for a sister who looked like she could be a contender on *America's Next Top Model*.

"No," he blurted. "No way. When I said I'd do anything

you want, I meant anything you want but that . . . and murder and extortion. Throw arson on that list too."

"Why not? Don't you care even the smallest bit about what happens to my—*our*—little sister?"

Walt gritted his teeth. "Of course I do. But stalking crosses the line, and you know it."

"Stalking?" Brad made a face, drawing back as if he'd been asked to host a Pampered Chef party. "I didn't say anything about stalking. All I want you to do is stick close to her and check out who she talks to . . . see where she goes . . . maybe find out what kind of guys are approaching her. That sort of thing. Then report it all back to me."

"Right. My mistake then."

Brad ran his hands over his head and sighed. "Look, you don't know what I've been living with, so give me a break here. Ever since she came back from college, she hasn't been dating the right kind of men, or even trying to date the right kind of men. She needs to spend time with someone who really deserves her."

For a brief moment Walt's heart stopped, but then as he looked into Brad's eyes he realized he'd misunderstood his friend's intent. Brad wasn't suggesting he date his sister at all. What a relief. How did something so bizarre as him dating Georgie even enter his mind anyway? He couldn't possibly want to date his best friend's sister.

To cover up the sudden awkwardness, Walt placed his hands over his heart with mock seriousness. "I'm touched, man. Really. But I can't—"

"I'm not talking about you, ding-dong. Sheesh. You're the last man on earth I'd want touching my sister. Or even *looking* at my sister that way."

"Gee, you really know how to make a guy feel special."

Brad's solemn expression finally cracked, and he laughed

out loud. "Aw, shut up. You know what I mean. You're like family to us. Besides, you're not even Georgie's type. I owe it to my parents to make sure she's settled in her life. They were always harping on me to take care of her because she's younger. And I never did. I always assumed it was their job, not mine. Well, now that they're gone, I'm finally going to step up to the plate. But I need your help. So, take her out and make sure she meets an okay guy for once. You know, be a brother to her. I'd be one myself, but if Georgie thinks I'm interfering in her life one more time, she'll flip out."

Walt set his jaw and tried to bank down his growing resentment. As crazy as it seemed, something irked him about not being considered Georgie's type, and he couldn't help wondering who exactly her brother thought was her type. But he called himself a fool and brushed the thought away.

Get your head together, stupid.

Walt rubbed the tips of his fingers along his eyebrows to ward off the King Kong headache he suddenly felt looming. "All right, wait a sec. Let me get this straight." If he could. Maybe he was the sane one after all, and Brad was the one who had the beer affecting him. "You want me to stalk—er, I mean—spend time with your sister so we can make sure she meets a decent guy? Is that right?"

Brad looked grim as he took a few seconds to think it over. "Yeah. That's pretty much it in a nutshell. What do you say?"

"I say you've completely lost your mind."

"No, I haven't. You don't understand. I really need you to do this for me. At least until she's married. No, scratch that. Until she at least gets her pharmacy license and gets settled with her job. How about that? Come on, I'd feel so much better about her going out knowing you were keeping an eye on her and steering her in the right direction."

Walt stared at the pleading—almost pathetic—appeal in

his friend's eyes. Poor Brad. The stress of being a policeman had finally gotten to him. The guy really had his sympathy for having an attractive, if overly impulsive, sister. But despite the things Brad had said, he was sure Georgie didn't need her hand held every waking moment. Walt had enough on his plate trying to get situated into town and handling the pharmacy while his uncle was out.

"Look," he said, with an apologetic grin, "I just can't do it. I'm sorry. You know I think of Georgie as my own sister, but I'll already be spending enough time with her at the pharmacy. Believe me, she'd get suspicious if I suddenly wanted to spend time with her outside of work too."

"No, man, she wouldn't. I think—"

"Listen to me, Brad. You don't have anything to worry about, okay? When I spoke to Georgie earlier today, she seemed to have quite a level head on her shoulders." If you took the whole condom fiasco out of the equation, that is. The woman could be reasoned with too. After all, she'd listened to him and hadn't entered that date contest. That was one crisis Brad wouldn't have to deal with.

Brad nodded, but looked as depressed as a six-year-old who'd just found out Santa had been run over by a disgruntled Rudolph. "All right," he said, playing with the tab on his beer can. "I guess you're right. Maybe I should give her a little more credit."

Brad hardly sounded grateful, but Walt forced himself not to give in. Instead he went into the kitchen and grabbed Brad another beer. It was the least he could do for a guy who had been there for him after his parents' divorce all those years ago. Walt appreciated him all the more and was sorry he couldn't help his friend out, but he had to draw the line at being Georgie's chaperone. His less-than-brotherly reaction to her earlier today told him if he didn't keep himself in check, he could get himself into some serious trouble. Which only meant the more distance he created away from "his little sister," the better off his friendship with Brad would be.

Georgie had lasted this long without a personal body-guard. Brad needed to chill out and stop worrying. She could run her own life. After all, what kind of problems could she possibly cause for herself?

The next morning Georgie woke before her alarm clock went off. She slowly stretched in bed, smiling at the Good Samaritan act she had performed for her brother last night. Brad was going to be so surprised when he found out about the date contest. Maybe if he won and got out a little more, he'd start acting more like a brother and less like a mother hen.

Georgie had stopped at Dee's house last night after work, and they'd celebrated their cleverness with Dee's husband over a glass of wine and some chocolate fondue. Surprisingly, Brad hadn't called to check up on her when she hadn't come home. He was acting less like a prison warden already. Maybe that was because he was too busy entertaining Walt Somers.

Georgie quickly buried her head under her pillow with a groan. Up until that point, she'd forgotten Walt was even staying with them. The man was probably putting his feet up on their coffee table, slurping up the last of the coffee, and thumbing through her new *Pharmacy Today* magazine right about now, just waiting for the opportunity to bring up their embarrassing encounter at the store yesterday. Suddenly, the idea of calling in sick became quite attractive. There was nothing better she wanted to do than to avoid Walt and his smug little "sit tight and don't do anything rash" comments.

She glanced at the clock. It was almost eight. Brad would

be at work by now since he was on day shifts this week at the police department, which meant he wouldn't be available to be a buffer between her and Walt. Oh well. No use putting off the inevitable. She climbed out of bed, gathered her hair into a high ponytail and sauntered out of her bedroom, hoping Walt had somehow found a place of his own already. Like that miracle was going to happen anytime soon.

Something smelled wonderful as soon as she stepped into the living room. Not the usual kind of wake-up call she was used to, not since her parents had died. Brad wasn't really a cook. But then again, neither was she. She supposed if she ever truly wanted to master the whole independent-woman principle she was so gung ho about, she would have to learn one day.

Her nose led her toward the kitchen where the aroma of eggs and bacon became stronger, and her stomach grumbled. She turned the corner, and that's when she saw Walt standing in front of the stove. And she froze.

He's hot. But it's only Walt, she tried to remind herself as she quickly realigned her gaze toward the white paint-cracked ceiling.

Yes, it was only Walt. The same Walt who'd locked her in the bathroom when she was eleven, then pretended to her family he hadn't seen her. Yeah, remember that, brain? That Walt. Besides, he was only frying eggs. A normal, everyday activity. No big deal.

She took a few deep, calming breaths. Confident with her regained composure, she allowed her gaze to slowly travel downward again.

Ah. See? No big deal. Walt cooking breakfast was no big deal. Except . . .

The man was cooking breakfast there in her kitchen wearing

low-cut jeans—very low-cut jeans—and nothing else. She tried to avert her eyes again, but something about the "nothing else" part of Walt's ensemble would not be ignored a second time. Not when his beefcake arms and bare broad chest looked as good as his did right then.

Down, girl.

Walt looked over at her and laughed. "I take it you're hungry."

She snapped her mouth shut and brushed by him to get to the refrigerator. She was being silly. It's not like she'd never seen a man without his shirt before. She lived in a beach resort for goodness sakes! Besides, Walt didn't look that perfect. His tan even looked a bit marred. Obviously, he was going a little easy on the sunscreen, due to the redness she saw around his navel, just above . . .

Oh, who was she kidding? Marred tan or not, Walt couldn't have looked more delicious if he were wearing those bacon and eggs he was so proficiently cooking.

"I'm not hungry at all," she said, proud of the way she didn't gargle her words due to the excess amount of drool in her mouth. "What you're cooking isn't on my diet anyway."

"Diet? Oh, come on. You shouldn't want to lose any weight. You look—" He turned and slid his gaze down her body and those scruffy cheeks of his turned bright pink, just as they had the other day at the store when she'd asked if he'd carried condoms. He jerked his head away and fumbled for a bagel. "Here"—he said, dangling it out for her—"be a good girl and eat something."

"Thanks," she said, plucking the bagel from his hand. She couldn't help but grin. There was something about an attractive thirty-one-year-old man blushing at her body that was kind of . . . cute.

"I'll only eat half. A woman's got to work a little harder than a girl to keep her figure, you know."

"Enjoy," he mumbled, turning away and giving his eggs a little flip. "You know, I shouldn't even be cooking for myself today."

She sliced her bagel and looked up. "What do you mean?"

"Don't you remember? You were supposed to cook me breakfast in exchange for not telling Brad about that whole condom mix-up. Forget about that already? I wonder what Brad would say when he hears about you trying to take over his job of law enforcement?"

Georgie put the knife down slowly—before she used it on something other than her bagel. She knew it. She knew Walt wouldn't let go what happened the other day. Reining in her anger, she poured herself a glass of juice and took a long, thoughtful sip.

Scratch all that likeable mumbo jumbo she'd just thought about him. Walt didn't want to play nice, and he seemed to take a sudden interest in making her life downright miserable. No matter how attractive he happened to be when he blushed, he was back on her hit list. "You know you're a rat, don't you?"

"You mentioned that yesterday."

"Well, I don't think it sunk in."

He chuckled, and she couldn't help but notice how the green in his hazel eyes lit up. "Okay, I'm sorry," he said. "Really I am. You're just so easy to rile up I can't resist teasing you. Whenever I see you, it's like when you were little."

When she was little.

Her heart sank. She turned away and went back to lightly buttering her bagel. It seemed as though everyone had a hard time accepting she wasn't the same little girl anymore, except

maybe a few friends. The little girl–sister box people kept putting her in was stifling. She wasn't sure how much more she could take of it. She needed out.

"Clay Hayes won't think of me as someone's little sister," she blurted, then bit her lip. She didn't know why she felt like throwing Clay Hayes in Walt's face again, or why she even felt she had something to prove to him in the first place, but the way Walt's cheek muscle twitched when she mentioned Clay's name satisfied a small sadistic part of her.

Walt carefully removed the frying pan from the burner and folded his arms. "Clay Hayes? I thought we already discussed him yesterday."

She shrugged her shoulders and tried for an innocent look. "I suppose we did."

"So why did you bring him up again then? You don't plan on trying to find out where his house is around here like one of his groupies, do you?"

"Of course not. I guess I just don't see what your problem is with me going out with a handsome TV star."

Walt clucked his tongue. "Oh, come on, Georgie. Take a look at yourself."

She continued to look at him instead. She assumed, like Dee, he wasn't being literal, so she resisted the urge to snap her head down and stare at her faded Red Sox sleep shirt.

"My problem is," he continued, "the guy is a good-looking—no, an okay-looking—television star, and you would be spending the day with him. Probably at his beach house. Alone. Catch my drift? Why do you think celebrities have contests like this? To prey on innocent starstruck women. It's a good thing you listened to me, and you didn't enter."

A good thing she listened to him?

Walt was doing it again, telling her what to do. How dare

he suggest the Clay Hayes contest was a fraud. She grabbed her bagel and took a huge bite, shooting him daggers with her eyes as she chewed. Who made him the end-all-be-all-date-contest authority anyway?

Her silence must have alerted him to what she had done, because his face took on a dubious expression. "Georgie, you . . . you didn't enter that contest, right?"

Would have served you right if I had. She swallowed and waited until she felt the bagel reach her stomach before answering, just to let him stew a little while longer. "No, as a matter of fact I did not enter—"

"Thank God," he breathed.

"—because I entered Brad."

Walt raised his eyebrows, staring at her as if she'd just told him she'd poisoned someone and needed suggestions on where to hide the body. When he finally became capable of moving again, he took her hand and shook it. "Well, it's been nice knowing you, because when Brad finds out he's going to skin you alive."

A twinge of alarm shot to the core of her stomach. Funny how she had only briefly thought Brad might have a negative reaction to the contest news. Hearing the words come from Walt's mouth made it sound like more than a good possibility her hide would be filleted, doused with gasoline, and set on fire. Eeww. She should have listened to her gut instincts. Darn her impetuousness! She only wanted to see her brother get out more and have some fun. Was that so wrong? Wrong enough to get skinned alive for?

"Oh my gosh, you're right! Don't tell him!" she begged. "He'll never have to know if he doesn't win anyway, right?"

"And what if he does win, Einstein?"

She scrunched her face and thought. There was still a slim chance Brad would appreciate her thoughtfulness, right? She had been so desperate to get her brother off her back, she hadn't bothered to think that far ahead.

"Well, if he wins . . . he'll be too ecstatic to yell at me?" she squeaked.

He made an annoying buzzer sound, and she flinched. "Wrong."

"Well, this is all your fault," she snapped, poking him in his bare chest with her index finger and trying not to notice how taut his muscles felt. "Maybe if you hadn't been so high-handed, ordering me to listen to you, and if you would have encouraged Brad to get out more instead of moping in front of the TV, I wouldn't have been forced to enter him."

"*Forced* to enter him?" Walt stepped back, rubbing his hands all over his face in frustration. "I've been in town less than thirty hours and you're blaming me? Oh, that's nice. That's just great. Honestly, Georgie, I don't know whether to laugh or to . . . to . . . ."

"Cry?" she supplied.

"Spank you."

She would have snorted, but the flicker of heat in Walt's eyes stopped her cold. There was something laced in his comment and expression that didn't have anything to do with treating her like a child. If she didn't know better, she would have thought in that moment Walt even regarded her as someone more than Brad's little sister. A phenomenon in its own right, considering the way everybody acted toward her lately. But then, Walt turned away with a chuckle, and she was certain she had made a mistake in thinking that. A big mistake.

"All right," he said, shaking his head, "seeing how this is somehow all my fault, I won't tell Brad what you did. I'm sure nothing will come out of it anyway. I mean, what are the odds, right? He'd probably have a better chance of winning the lottery."

Yeah, the odds were bad. Part of Walt's words relieved her, and also depressed her at the same time. She had hoped the contest would be the perfect diversion for her brother and would get her some breathing room. "I guess you're right. But I really wanted him to go on that date. I felt so sorry for him."

"You felt sorry for Brad so you entered him in a contest to win a date with a TV star?" He rolled his eyes toward the ceiling. "I hope you never get any of those compassionate feelings toward me."

She gave him a tight-lipped smile. "Don't worry. You're more than safe."

With her stomach now in knots, she tossed her bagel on the counter. "The only reason I entered Brad was because I think he's lonely. He needs someone to occupy his thoughts. With the way he's been overly concerned with me, I'd say he has way too much time on his hands. His actions are not only affecting my life but his too." She bit her lip and hesitated a moment more before letting Walt in on her plan B. "You know, um, I was even hoping, um, since you were back in town that—"

"Wait. Don't tell me," he said with a chuckle. "You want me to take Brad out and maybe see that he meets a nice girl."

Her eyes widened. "Wow. How did you know?"

"Call me psychic."

"I suppose it's better than some of the other names I could call you."

A wide grin spread across his face. "Well, well, now who's acting like old times? You know, I could complain about how you talk to me as well. Ever since I came to town, you've been treating me as if I were still fifteen and running over your Barbie with my dirt bike."

"*You* did that?"

Walt's smug expression suddenly turned guilty, and he cleared his throat. "Uh, I can't quite remember. Hey, it might have been Brad now that I think about it. Or some other jerk he was friends with. Tim Clark, I think. You know, it's all a big blur to me now."

She cracked a smile. "Sure, it is."

Despite what she knew he'd done all those years ago, his lighthearted mood was so infectious and charming she laughed and lightly punched him in the arm. But as soon as she started to draw back her hand, he caught her off guard by reaching out and taking hold of it in his own.

"Uh, listen, Georgie," he said, thoughtfully studying their joined hands for a moment. "If I was the one who had run over your Barbie, well, I'm sorry. Even if we weren't friends back then, I would like us to be friends now. Not only for Brad's sake, but for the pharmacy's sake too. I was a difficult kid—kind of mad at the world because of my mom leaving. But it still wasn't a very nice thing to do, especially to my best friend's sister."

She stared at their joined hands too, trying to decide if she liked this new side of Walt or not. The seriousness he used combined with his deep, velvety voice had a strange effect on her heart rate, and she suddenly didn't know how to act. For all her talk about wanting to be treated as a grown woman, the only thing she could think of now was running and hiding under her covers.

She pulled her hand away from his grasp and fervently tried to switch the mood back to one she felt safe with. "It—it's not a big deal. So, how about it? Are you going to start acting like a real friend and stop being such a stick in the mud?"

Walt shrugged. "Okay. Why not? I'll take Brad out Saturday night. I could use a little fun myself."

Yes! Saturday was perfect. That would give her three days

to find a date and maybe go out herself. Her own social life was already looking up. "You mean it?" she asked eagerly.

"Sure. But on one condition."

Ugh. And just like that, her good mood became crushed, much like her old Barbie's head.

Here we go. She knew Walt was acting too good to be true. This was it. This was where the true Walt would come out, and he would make her promise him breakfast in bed for a month, maybe even a year. Maybe he'd even want her firstborn and her firstborn's firstborn.

"You've got to come out with us too," he finished.

She blinked up at him, thinking she overestimated his guilt for mowing down her old Barbie. Why would Walt want her hanging around a boys' night out? That didn't sound like such a hot idea. Having his younger sister around wouldn't be conducive to Brad relaxing and meeting a woman.

"Go out with the two of you?" she asked. "Oh. I don't know. I . . ." *Think, brain! Think!*

Walt leaned in, looking vaguely amused at her uneasiness. "What's the matter?" he asked. "We haven't seen each other in years. It'll be a great opportunity for us to catch up and get better acquainted with each another."

Better acquainted with Walt? She didn't think that was such a hot idea either.

She dropped her gaze away so she could think better, but her mind stalled when she ended up with an eyeful of his chest hair. Not only was she not sure she liked this new personality of Walt's, but she wasn't sure she liked this new dress code of his. Handsome, kind, and shirtless was not a combination that was going to resolve this sudden infatuation she was feeling toward him anytime soon.

She drew a shaky breath and looked up. "Well, uh . . . as a matter of—"

"Great." He beamed, and the corners of his eyes crinkled in a way-too-appealing manner. "It's a date then."

"Oh. Yeah, that sounds . . . great." A date. With Walt.

And her brother.

No, not great. And not exactly the kind of date she was looking for. But maybe this was what she needed to get a guy like Walt out of her system. Ever since she'd seen him, her body responded to him in ways she wasn't used to. It worried her.

Whenever she'd gone on dates or hung around attractive men in the past, she'd always been able to have a great time and keep her emotions in check. But when she looked at Walt, it was an entirely different matter. The last thing she wanted was to be drawn to someone like him. He was just like her brother—overprotective, domineering, someone who saw her as a person unable to make intelligent decisions. Yikes. No, she didn't want that. She had met and even dated a few of those Neanderthal type know-it-alls in college. That was enough for her. She wanted a man who saw she had a good head on her shoulders and saw her for what she really was—not just a little sister who needed protecting.

She was sure that once Walt and Brad were together, they'd go back to their old ways of treating her, and she'd be reminded of all the reasons why she should ignore her physical reaction to Walt. Then she could go back to concentrating on a more important matter—finding her brother a woman.

Chapter Five

After four days at the store, Walt was still finding things he could improve upon. He hadn't anticipated putting this much work into it so soon, but once he had a chance to oversee the pharmacy without his uncle in the way, Walt's business instincts automatically took over.

Expired drugs had already been pulled from the shelves, but prescriptions from four years ago still needed to be boxed and filed away. The antiquated way of keeping their books had to be updated to a better computer system. The good news was the video surveillance camera he had ordered would be in next week. He hoped they'd at least be able to figure out how the condom thefts had happened and prevent any other shoplifting. Now if he could just come up with a way to keep their sales from slipping further, he and his uncle might actually be able to hold on to their business for the foreseeable future.

Walt decided to give his eyes a break from all the paperwork he'd been perusing and checked his watch. Eleven fifty-five. The next technician was scheduled to arrive any minute, and it happened to be one Georgiana Louise Mayer.

He sighed.

Maybe it was his imagination but it seemed as though Georgie had been avoiding him these last few days. Fortunately for her, he'd been pretty busy doing paperwork in the stock room. Randall had been understanding enough to do pharmacist duty all week so that Walt could look over the business aspects of the store more closely. Today would be the first time she and Walt would really be working together.

A small part of him even looked forward to it.

"Hey, Walt"—Dee called, breaking into his thoughts—"I need you to come over here and check this drug interaction before I print the label."

Walt pushed Georgie out of his mind and approached the computer. After he typed in his initials, he began flipping through the screens until he located the interaction. Dee kept courteously silent as he reviewed the potential problem, but he could tell she was anxious to speak to him about something by the way he heard her fidgeting behind him.

"Okay, I'm going to write a note on Miss Hanley's prescription bag to remind you that I want to talk to her about how to take these pills before she takes them home." When he was met with silence, he turned around and looked at her. "Got that, Dee?"

"Sure, no problem," she said, but she had a glimmer in her eyes that made him uncomfortable. "And speaking of no problems . . . how's living with Brad and Georgie going?"

Walt avoided her gaze and finished writing his note on Miss Hanley's bag. How was living with Brad and Georgie going? Living with Brad was fine. Living with Georgie, well, that was another story. True, he'd barely seen her but those few brief times had been hellish enough. Especially when she sashayed around the condo in nothing but skimpy Red Sox nightshirts.

There was a limit to how many cold showers a man could take in one morning.

He played with the folded-up edges of the prescription bag and hesitated answering another moment, hoping his response wouldn't come out sounding like the outright lie it was. "Living with them is great. Why?"

"Oh, I don't know. I thought I picked up on some kind of vibe between you and Georgie the other day." Dee gave him a tight smile and pried the prescription from his fingers. "I guess it must have been my imagination."

"Yeah, I guess so," he muttered.

Vibes. Yeah, right. Women see what they want to see. There weren't any vibes going on between him and Georgie. How could there be? He may have thought Georgie was very attractive, but that didn't mean there were any vibes going around. Vibes would mean he was interested in her. And that wouldn't be right. Getting involved with her would muck up his employee-employer relations. More importantly, his friendship with her brother. He wasn't about to test its loyalty. Brad's friendship meant too much to him.

Dee cocked her head. "You know, you don't sound like the same Walt Somers my brothers used to talk about when they were in high school. Does that strangely noncommittal answer mean that Georgie is out of luck and you're already involved with someone else?"

"No," he said with a sigh. "There's no one else. I haven't had the time to think about dating lately."

"Ah-ha, the plot thickens," she said, grinning. "This is getting better than any Clay Hayes show I could be watching now." She plopped down on one of the stools nearby and made herself more comfortable. "So, allow me to analyze, if you will. A good-looking guy like yourself has no ex-girlfriends in the background or hot prospects on the horizon? What's the matter with single women today? Next to Brad, you seem to be the most eligible bachelor around." Her eyes narrowed as she suddenly wagged her finger at him. "You have any funky skeletons in your closet we should know about?"

"Uh, no. No skeletons in the closet. Just your average hometown boy who likes to keep his love life an off limit topic from town gossip."

"Hmm," she said, nodding and tapping her chin. "I get it. Butt out, right? Oh, pooh. That's no fun."

"What's no fun?" Georgie rushed into the pharmacy just then, with flushed cheeks and those long red curls of hers kinking and swaying against her shoulders like festive Mardi Gras streamers. "Sorry I'm a little late, Walt," she said all out of breath. "Couldn't find my lab jacket. I guess I'll just wear Al's over there, if that's okay with you."

Walt could only nod as the scent of oranges and flowers floated around him as she dashed toward the coatrack. He wondered if all his employees smelled as good and he just hadn't noticed yet. He stood there, transfixed by her scent. Then his breath caught in his throat as she unbuttoned and slowly peeled off her sweater coat. *Oh, crap!* He realized he was doing it again—ogling her like a sex-starved teenager.

Were these the vibes Dee had alluded to? Or was he losing his mind? Georgie wasn't doing a striptease in the pharmacy, but the way his body was responding she might as well have been. He quickly caught himself and closed his mouth before Dee got any further suspicions.

So much for not being interested. Brad would slug him for sure, if he knew where his mind was heading. Georgie wasn't even wearing anything provocative—a light-blue blouse and a plain black skirt that fell to just above her knees—yet he still couldn't look away. He noticed Georgie had very nice legs, and although Al's pharmacy coat was at least two sizes too big, it wasn't anywhere near long enough to cover them up.

He was obviously in for a long night.

"What's no fun?" Georgie repeated, shoving some pens in her pocket and walking over to them.

Dee jerked her thumb at Walt. "He doesn't want to talk about how such a prime specimen like himself has managed to elude the marriage market for so long."

Georgie batted her eyes. "I could probably venture a guess or two."

When Walt didn't respond to her jibe, she felt a small stab of guilt for automatically poking fun of him. Customers approached the register, and Dee hurried over to wait on them. A prescription came through the fax, and Georgie went over to the computer to type a label. Unfortunately, she had to force herself to concentrate on what she was reading.

Well, why wasn't Walt seeing anyone? The man certainly had attractive attributes, if you went for the hot, blond, surfer type. He wasn't a workaholic. He obviously wasn't a playboy either. And, unlike Brad, Walt couldn't be distracted from meddling into his sibling's life. So why was there no girlfriend in the picture? There must have been droves of women dying of heartbreak when he'd moved from Philadelphia to Maritime City.

Not that she was interested in Walt's love life for any reason other than simple curiosity. She just figured that maybe she should get to know Walt a little better. For Brad's sake. Walt did seem a little different now than when she'd known him all those years ago. She hated it when people made assumptions about her, but here she had pigeonholed someone else in the exact same way. Maybe Dee was right, and she should give him a small break.

Walt came over and stood next to her, waiting for the
label to print out so he could compare what she typed out
to what the actual prescription said. This was her moment.
While Dee was at the register, Georgie couldn't resist taking the opportunity to satisfy her own notions about his
attitude toward relationships—and maybe about the man
himself.

She hit the ENTER key and turned toward him. "Is it
because you feel suffocated?"

His eyebrows shot up. "Excuse me?"

She sighed. The words flew out of her mouth before she
could stop them. Sometimes she wished she could lasso her
tongue. "Uh, you know, the reason you aren't in a relationship. Is it because you . . . you know, feel that way?"

"You mean suffocated?" he asked with an amused grin.

"Yeah." She bit her lip and looked away. Great. Now he
was laughing at her. But way in the back of her mind suffoca-
tion was her biggest fear, which was why she always wanted
her dealings with the opposite sex to be light and breezy.
Less chance for anyone to dictate how she'd run her life.
Once she became independent from her brother and lived on
her own, she didn't want anyone interfering with what she did.
Maybe her fear was irrational, she wasn't sure. Until now,
she'd never even spoken about that fear aloud.

He must have sensed her anxiety because he closed the
gap between them and his expression softened. "No," he
said gently. "I've never felt—I don't feel suffocated. What's
the matter, Georgie? Why are you asking about this?"

"Oh, I . . . I don't know." She gave a little shrug, trying to
shake off his concern, and went back to typing the few prescriptions Dee had set down next to her. She felt foolish for
voicing her question to someone like Walt and tried for a dif-

ferent mood. "I'm sorry, Walt. I guess I'm just surprised that you aren't with someone. You seem like the kind of man who should have a nice girlfriend."

Staggering backward, Walt clutched his chest. "Whoa, be still my heart, was that a kind word I heard from you? Maybe there's a chance we can be friends after all."

"Well, I *am* sorry you don't have a girlfriend. If you did, you could have stayed with her and you wouldn't be living with Brad and me." She glanced over at him and laughed when she saw his face fall.

"I should have seen that one coming," he murmured, shaking his head.

"You must be slipping in your old age, so I'll cut you some slack. Dementia can't be that far off for you, so it's a good thing I've already taken it upon myself to do some thinking as far as the business is concerned."

He didn't bother stifling a groan as he snatched the prescription label from the printer. "Look, Georgie, no offense, but I was district supervisor for six years in Philadelphia. I think I can come up with some of my own ideas to help the pharmacy. Thanks anyway, but I've got it covered."

"Okay," she challenged. "If you're such a smarty corporate business man, why don't you run an idea by Dee and me, and we can give you our opinion on it?"

Walt rubbed his chin and let a few moments pass while he seemed to think about it, but when no impromptu ideas came forth, he clamped his lips and stared her down with a heated glint.

She smiled smugly and continued to wait for an answer.

Dee came over with a few more prescriptions and set them on the counter by Georgie. "Mrs. Johnson is coming back to pick those up tomorrow, so no rush. Oh, and she wants someone to show her a good glucose monitor to buy when she comes back too."

"Thanks," Georgie said, picking up a prescription and fanning herself with it. "Actually, Mrs. Johnson's request plays a part in the idea I came up with. Would you care to hear it now, Walt? Or are you still trying to come up with your own plan?"

"Okay, fine," he grumbled. "Let's hear it."

"Great. Here's what I was thinking. We could set up a mini diabetes expo in the center of the store. You know, set up a table with free brochures and sample products. We could have an extra pharmacist available all day just to talk to customers about their disease and how they're managing it. Maybe we could even suggest customers bring in a chart of their daily blood sugar levels for a free analysis. Oh, and we could give away a free blood sugar monitor as a door prize. What do you think about something like that?" She held her breath and waited.

Walt's brows pulled together as he rubbed the back of his neck. "A diabetes expo, huh?"

"Uh-huh. And at the risk of tooting my own horn, I think it would be a wonderful service to provide to the community. This little store could fill a niche that those big corporate drugstores can't provide: genuine concern for the health of our customers."

"Hey, Georgie, that's pretty good," Dee commented.

Georgie smiled then looked anxiously at Walt, who seemed to be still considering the idea. He was staring at the floor. She thought she heard him utter a few grunts, but then he suddenly looked up and his lips slid into a breathtaking smile. "All right, Georgie. I might have to agree with Dee here. It is a pretty good idea."

"Oh my gosh. You really think so?"

He chuckled. "Yeah, actually I don't think I could have come up with a better plan myself. A diabetes expo sounds like the perfect solution to get customers in the door as well as show them that we care about them. You know something, Georgie? You really surprise me. Who knew you'd be beauty and brains all in one package."

He sounded so sincere she wanted to hug him. Her idea *was* good. She knew it was. But it was nice to have her idea validated anyway. Walt even looked right into her eyes when he spoke that last part about having beauty and brains, proving his sincerity all the more. For once, someone really appreciated the advice she had to give.

Only . . . maybe he appreciated the advice a little too much?

Because something suddenly changed in the way Walt was looking at her just then, and she had to swallow hard. His gaze took on an almost seductive quality as his hand moved to her shoulder. He moved even closer, and she caught that delicious light pine scent of his aftershave. Her heart began to hammer in a nervous rhythm. For one brief crazy second, it looked as though Walt was going to kiss her. Right there in the pharmacy.

Right there in front of Dee.

Right there in front of Mrs. Johnson—and any other customers still lingering in the store.

Oh, Lord.

The real problem was she wasn't as appalled at the idea as she had hoped. Walt's lips looked so soft. Almost too soft for a man. Which probably meant he'd kissed a lot of women in his life—women who wore extra-moisturizing lip gloss. A man who seemed to be so popular with women couldn't be all that bad. Could he? For some reason, she desperately wanted to find out if that theory rang true, so being the complete hussy she was, she decided to help him out and leaned in too.

Then the phone rang. And they blinked at one another.
The moment ended.

The phone rang again, and Dee twisted in between them to answer it. "Somers Shore Pharmacy," she chirped into the receiver as if she hadn't almost witnessed her boss and her friend about to make out right there in front of her. Dee grabbed a pen and paper and started jotting down prescription numbers.

Georgie moved away from the computer—and away from Walt's hand on her shoulder—to give herself some air. That was close. She wasn't sure what had just happened there, but she thought she'd almost kissed Walt Somers. Her brother's best friend. Her new boss. In the pharmacy.

But she couldn't help herself. Her lips had felt like they'd been caught in some invisible tractor beam. Oh my gosh, yes. Aliens or some other life force had to have been involved. That was the only way to explain her reaction. Otherwise, she'd have to admit that she actually wanted to jump her brother's best friend.

She glanced at Walt, who was looking everywhere but at her. She rubbed her temples and hoped something witty would magically pop into her head before Dee hung up the phone. The silence between them was deafening. She had to say something to Walt—anything—to break up the tension radiating around them or she was going to scream.

Luckily, Walt cleared his throat and spoke first. "Uh, again, great work, Georgie. We should start putting your plan into action as soon as possible. Before summer hits. I'll go see if I can find the numbers of some of the pharmaceutical sales representatives in our area. Maybe they'd be willing to give us some free samples and things we can give away to customers who show up for the expo." He immediately swung around toward the filing cabinets and started digging through its contents.

Georgie stood motionless, staring at his back like some jackanape. That near-kiss had vanished so quickly she thought she might have imagined the whole thing—until she noticed the paper Walt pulled out and was studying.

It was upside down.

Oh, great. She obviously had him spooked. The poor guy. What a dope she was. Walt had given her idea about the diabetes expo serious consideration. He had treated her as a professional equal. Then she almost ruined everything and kissed him. He and Brad would have had a good laugh about that too, much to her expense. One little compliment and she went into full-force infatuation mode.

Not a good way to exhibit maturity.

She snuck another peek at Walt. He was still reading his paper upside down. She had to smile.

Dee was right about another thing. Walt was sure fine to look at. Georgie couldn't help but appreciate the way his lab coat molded nicely over his wide shoulders and back, and she experienced a little tingle of awareness again.

Hmm. Infatuation mode was pretty hard to distinguish from lust mode. But she supposed there was no harm in enjoying the view. For now. At least, until she could decide if this infatuation with Walt was a good or bad thing. Maybe after their dinner tomorrow night with Brad, she'd have the answer.

Chapter Six

I thought you said Georgie was going to meet us here?"

Brad tipped his chin hello to a passing blond, whose smile at the mere acknowledgment could have lit up all of Las Vegas, before he answered. "Yeah, she'll be here. But I think she said something about getting her toenails painted or something before coming over."

Walt lifted his beer and took a healthy swallow. The last thing he needed was to be reminded of any body parts on his friend's sister. Georgie had adorable toes—not that he had a toe fetish or stared at her feet often—but when Georgie was in a room, it was hard not to notice everything about her. Toes, ears, eyes, hair, legs . . . lips. He had just proved that point yesterday when he'd almost kissed her in the pharmacy.

What had he done, thinking he could invite her out like this and prove he could still treat her like he always had? This friendly dinner get-together idea wasn't going to work at all—not if he wanted his relationship with Georgie to remain platonic.

Why couldn't he just remind himself that Georgie would

bring nothing but complications to his life? She was like family. He was her boss. Her brother owned several guns . . .

Walt looked back at Brad and forced a smile. "Toenails painted, huh? I hope she's not getting all dolled up just for us."

Brad snorted as he picked up a menu. "Get real."

"Oh, right. What I meant to say is that Georgie is a natural beaut—She's very attract—Uh, she doesn't strike me as the type of woman who gets her nails done on a regular basis." Walt mentally rolled his eyes at himself. He needed to get his act together before he went and blurted out in front of Brad that he had the major hots for his only sister.

"Nah, she isn't the high-maintenance type," Brad said. "I can guarantee you if she is getting dolled up, it's not for us. I'm sure my sister's got some ulterior motive. I just hope she doesn't attract any more of those loser types I've had to get rid of. It's getting to be a bit of a hobby, one that's going to send me to the grave if she doesn't start becoming more discriminate."

A moan from the bar area had them both craning their necks to see the wide-screen TV around which most of the men in the place had congregated. After a few minutes of baseball highlight reports, Brad pointed toward the crowd around the barstools. "Hey, what do you think about him? You think that guy over there would be a good candidate for Georgie?"

He followed his friend's gaze where it had settled on a tall, dark-haired, good-looking guy in a gray business suit. The man reminded Walt of a young Alec Baldwin. "No way in hell."

Brad's eyebrows shot up. "You're kidding, right? That guy looks like a normal guy with a halfway decent job, and I don't see a wedding band on his finger. What's wrong with him?"

Walt thought about that for a second. Unfortunately, he couldn't think of a thing. Oh, hell. There wasn't anything wrong with him. On the surface, that is.

Walt studied the guy with a little more scrutiny this time. He still couldn't find anything physically wrong with him—besides being a bit of a fancy boy with that Brooks Brothers shirt-and-tie combo. There wasn't a scratch on him either, not even a stray eyebrow hair in sight. The man looked charming, successful, and clean-cut.

Then again, so had Ted Bundy.

That settled it. You could never be too sure about men, case in point was himself. But especially if they were talking about a man who was going to be with Georgie. There had to be higher standards set, and Walt was just the man to help his friend set them. Way high. But first, he had to break it to Brad in a means he'd understand. Lay out his case in a level-headed manner. Friend to friend. Man to man.

"I don't like him," Walt blurted, then inwardly cringed. *Oooh, nice manly explanation, moron. Gee, a four-year-old could've had a better response.*

Judging by the look on Brad's face, he'd evidently thought so too. "You don't like him? You know him or something?"

"Uh, well, no. Not . . . not exactly."

"Okay, then let's go over there and strike up a conversation with him and see what kind of guy he is. If he seems decent enough, we'll introduce him to Georgie. Sound like a plan?" Brad didn't wait for an answer and started to stand.

"No!" Walt cleared his throat, then lowered his voice. "I mean, I don't think that's such a hot idea. I don't know him personally, but I know the business-executive type. I dealt with them in Philadelphia. Georgie wouldn't like a man like that. Those kinds of guys are into themselves and are not the friendly sort. Very cold." He rubbed his upper arms for effect, just in case Brad had forgotten what the definition of cold was, and added an exaggerated, "Brrrr."

Brad shot a dubious glance over at Mr. Wall Street again. The man was smiling pleasantly, shaking hands with Pete the bartender, and he was getting a few slaps on the back from some nearby customers. Obviously, the man was popular too.

Definitely *not* Georgie's type.

"Are you sure about that?" Brad asked. "Pete seems to like him. Don't you think we should at least check the guy out and give him the benefit of the doubt? He has to be better than some of the guys Georgie's been meeting."

Walt shook his head, thinking if he were Pinocchio his nose would be enjoying the clean crisp mountain air of the Swiss Alps right about then. "No. Trust me. I'm sensing something's up with him, and it's not good. You'll be sorry. The guy shouldn't even be in the running."

Brad sat back and frowned. "Wow. Jeez, I'm glad you were here then. That really saved me some time."

"Happy to help." Unable to look his friend in the eye another second, Walt glanced away and across the bar just in time to see Georgie standing at the entrance on tiptoe, scanning the crowded room. He wasn't the only one that had seen her come in. Mr. Wall Street's attention suddenly shifted and lingered at the front door too.

Walt gritted his teeth. *Back off, buddy.*

As much as he felt like poking the guy's eyes out right at the moment, Walt couldn't exactly blame him. Not with the way Georgie looked tonight in that aqua tank top and those tight white jeans, clinging to the short curve of her hips. Used to seeing her in baggy sleep shirts and oversized lab coats, Walt couldn't help but appreciate how tiny but well-proportioned a body she had.

Oddly enough, Georgie's body wasn't the first thing Walt had noticed about her tonight; it was her eyes. With her wild hair pulled back and gathered in a low ponytail, she drew more attention to her face and her beautiful eyes appeared bluer than ever. Georgie looked sweet and sexy and could have been considered a walking oxymoron—the girl-next-door and a Victoria's Secret model all wrapped up in one.

Walt's mouth went dry. Then he realized, like every other man in the bar—minus Brad—that he was gawking. Well, there was no doubt about it. Walt wanted her. Georgie was all woman now, and he couldn't help but think of her in an all-male way.

God help him—and his friendship with her brother.

Walt stood and waved her over. Her face brightened when she saw him, and she waved back, making a beeline for their table. "Hey, guys," she chirped, as she took a seat between Walt and her brother. Her fruity scent of mandarin oranges and cranberry permeated the air around them, causing Walt's heart rate to spike further. "Sorry I'm a little late," she added sheepishly.

"You're more than a little late," Brad shot. "Sheesh. What are you trying to do, starve me to death?"

Georgie looked at her watch in disgust. "I'm fifteen minutes late. Hardly enough time to have you die from hunger. Besides, if I really wanted to starve you I'd delete the pizza delivery number you have on your cell phone speed dial."

Brad slapped his menu down on the table. "That's not funny, Georgie. I work long hours so I don't always have time to—"

"Oh, please. I've seen you order pizza for breakfast. Your arteries must be so clog—"

"Children, children," Walt interrupted, hiding a smile. "We're in a public place. Maybe we could all just decide what we want to order, and you two can settle your dietary differences in private later."

Georgie cast a pointed look at her brother. "Fine. I'm going to have the Greek salad with a vinaigrette dressing on the side."

"Good for you and your arteries," Brad muttered.

Walt chuckled at their banter. At least some things hadn't changed. Their sparring helped ease the tension he felt about being around Georgie tonight. That is, until she stood up and her gold-hoop belly ring caught the direct line of his vision. He turned his head and tried to blink away the image from his mind.

Oh, hell. She even made his eyelids sweat.

"It's a little quiet in here tonight," she said, her gaze traveling around to the bar area. "I think I'll go put some quarters in the jukebox."

Walt looked over to where the jukebox was—three feet away from Mr. Wall Street—and felt the blood between his ears grow hot and thick. Wasn't this just a dandy prospect? There was no way he was about to let her go and parade herself around like some fawn in front of a hungry lion. He felt a surge of protectiveness toward her, but this time he knew it was for purely selfish reasons.

"Do you have to do that right now?" Walt asked her. "I mean, you just sat down. Wait a few minutes." *Until Mr. Wall Street goes home. Or until I can find a parka to cover you up with.* "At least wait until you order."

To Walt's dismay, the waitress who had been MIA since he and Brad had first sat down at their table suddenly materialized.

"Are you ready, or do you need more time?" the waitress asked, staring down at her spiral order book. Then the pretty brunet glanced up and her brown eyes brightened when she took in her customers. "Oh, for goodness sake! I didn't even realize it was you guys."

"Hi, Kendall!" Georgie beamed at her. "I forgot you'd be working tonight."

"When am I *not* working?" Kendall rolled her eyes with a smirk then turned to Brad and poked him in the shoulder. "Hey, what's up with you? No hello? I noticed you haven't talked to me much since I started dating Jake. Are you mad at me because I'm now consorting with the enemy?"

Brad smiled at her joke, but it didn't quite reach his eyes. "I have nothing against Jake. It's not his fault he chose to be a firefighter instead of something respectable like a law-enforcing public-safety providing police officer."

"Oh, pish posh," Kendall said, waving her little notebook in the air. "I'll never understand why the fire and police departments can't get along."

Georgie snorted. "Probably has something to do with too much floating testosterone and not enough territory to mark. Oh, by the way," she said, gesturing to her right, "Kendall, this is Walt Somers. He's just moved into town. He's co-owner of Somers Shore Pharmacy with Al."

"Walt Somers? Oh, you're related to Al?"

Walt nodded. "Al's my uncle."

"Well, what a small world. It's a real pleasure." Kendall smiled and held out her hand. Walt took it and was surprised to find quite a grip behind such a delicate feature. "Georgie's new boss, huh? I never get bosses that look as good as you do," she added with a good-natured wink.

"Yeah, well, looks can be deceiving," Georgie said, batting her eyelashes in Walt's direction. "Hey, you shouldn't be noticing anyone's boss anyway. Remember? You have Jake."

Kendall slapped her forehead and laughed. "Oh, that reminds me! Georgie, what happened to you last weekend? You promised me you were going to come in here with your new date."

Georgie's smiled faded, then she shot Brad a cross look. "Yeah, well, that *was* the idea. Unfortunately, the plans I had took an erroneous and unavoidable detour."

"Oh." Kendall looked unsure for a moment, but then her lips broke out into a giddy grin as she bounced on her toes. "Well, the reason I asked is because I wanted to share my good news with you." Unable to contain her excitement for one millisecond longer, she flung out her left hand, exposing a small diamond engagement ring.

Georgie squealed and jumped out of her seat, flinging herself at her friend. Walt took a sip of his beer as he watched the two girls hug and jump with joy, as if they both hit the Mega Million and learned George Clooney would be delivering the check. Amused at the women's gushy display, Walt looked over at Brad to make a smart comment, but he quickly held himself back. At that moment, his friend looked anything but amused.

"I'm going to the john," Brad announced as he stood.

Neither woman took interest in his movement, or his sudden, inappropriate declaration. The two broke away from their embrace and continued to hold hands as Kendall began to explain in detail how Jake had popped the question. Brad shifted around them without bothering to send them a second glance and mumbled out a short "congrats" as he stormed away.

Kendall stopped her story, and her hurt gaze followed Brad across the room. "What's the matter with Brad? I thought he'd be happy for me."

Walt didn't feel it his place to enlighten Kendall on the diverse reactions men and women usually had on the announcement of engagements. Although, considering this woman was supposed to be a friend, he had to admit Brad's response was a little out of the ordinary. And a little interesting. He wondered if his surly mood had anything to do with the pretty waitress suddenly being taken off the dating market.

"Oh, don't mind him," Georgie said with a huff. "For some reason, since he doesn't have a life he's sour on everyone else's happiness. The man needs a love life, pronto. Thank goodness I decided not to wait any longer to do something about it."

Walt rolled his eyes and groaned. "Oh, man, not this again."

Kendall didn't look exactly thrilled with the idea either. "You're going to fix Brad up? Do you really think that's wise?"

"Yes."

"No," Walt blurted at the same time.

Kendall laughed. "Oh dear. I'm sorry, but I think Walt's right. Brad doesn't strike me as a person who needs or even *wants* a girlfriend. Whenever he comes in here, he's always by himself. He never tries to talk to any women. And believe me, there have been many who've tried."

Georgie planted both fists on her slim hips, and Walt struggled not to fixate on the subtle feminine curve of them. "No offense, but I think I know my brother better than you two."

Walt shook his head. "Yeah, right. You think you know your brother? You entered him in a date contest with a complete stranger. How's that for knowing him?"

"Oh. Well, that might have been one momentary lapse in judgment. But Rae Roberts isn't exactly a complete stranger. Thousands—millions—of people know her from her TV show."

Kendall's eyes bugged out and her bow-shaped lips suddenly formed a giant circle. "You entered Brad in the Win a Date with Clay and Rae contest? Oh dear. I don't think he's going to like that very much."

Georgie's face almost turned green. "Look, can we all just drop the discussion of the contest. I admit that was a mistake on my part, but there's nothing I can do about it now. So let's put our heads together and see if we can find Brad a single woman in this town—preferably before he comes back from the bathroom."

"Too late," Kendall said, motioning behind Georgie with her chin. "He's on his way back now."

Walt downed the rest of his beer and was ready to ask Kendall to bring him a few more in anticipation of the night's events. Hanging around two siblings vying to fix each other up was starting to make him crazy. Or maybe it was just Georgie who was making him crazy.

When Brad came back to the table, he didn't sit down. "Hey, sorry to do this to you guys, but I think I'm going to head out now."

Walt frowned. "Head out? But your sister just got here."

"Yeah, I just got here," Georgie echoed. "At least eat something. You just said you were starving."

Brad glanced at Kendall then shook his head. "I'm not really hungry anymore. My shoulder's been acting up. I think I need to go home and ice it."

Georgie immediately jumped to his side and started fingering his arm and shoulder area. Walt watched her hands move deftly over her brother and briefly thought about faking an injury himself, hoping he could get lucky enough to get that kind of TLC too. Yeah, right. Like that would ever happen.

"You have a shoulder problem?" she asked Brad. "You never told me that. Where does it hurt? Should I stop at the pharmacy and get you some ibuprofen?"

"No, that's all right, Georgie," he said, removing her hands from his shoulder. "We got plenty of medicine at home. I probably did something to it directing traffic today. I'll be fine." He gave her a weak smile. "You and Walt stay and have fun."

Before anyone had a chance to protest further, Brad had turned and was already walking out the door.

Georgie sank back into her chair, worry etched all over her pretty features. "How odd. Walt, did Brad mention a shoulder problem to you today?"

"Uh, no. But I don't think he's exactly the sort of guy to complain."

"Hmm. I don't know. You haven't lived with him for as long as I have. For a grown man, he can sometimes be one hundred and eighty-five pounds of pure baby."

Walt hid a smile. Although she tried to hide it behind her smart-alecky comments and her complaints about Brad, Georgie had a true tenderhearted side to her that Walt admired. Despite Brad and Georgie's constant bickering, she really did care a great deal about her brother. Walt even felt a tinge of jealousy toward their relationship. He often wondered if his relationship with his father would have been different—if they would've been closer—if he had a sibling to share the grief over his mom leaving. At least Brad and his parents had been around then to help him through it. They had been a wonderful support to him.

Kendall snapped her order book closed and sighed. "I'm sorry, guys. It seems as though my big news was an instant party killer to your night out. I'll give you two some time to decide whether you want to stay or not. Pete's waving me over, so I'll be back in a sec."

When Kendall headed back toward the bar area, Georgie turned to Walt with a shy smile. "So . . ."

"Yeah. So . . . ," he repeated, wondering what to do next. He'd hoped to get to know Georgie better in the confines of her brother in a nice platonic atmosphere. He hadn't counted on spending any real alone time with her.

"We might as well order, don't you think?" she asked

sheepishly. "I guess it'd be kind of crazy not to stay and eat something."

Crazier to stay, he thought, thinking he'd probably enjoy her company just a little too much for his own good.

She frowned, mistaking his silence as not wanting to stay, and she stood. "Yeah, I guess it's a pretty stupid idea. We should just go home too."

Before another rationalization entered his mind, he blurted, "No, stay!" She froze and her eyes widened. Even he was a little surprised at the desperation in his voice. But there was no turning back now.

He grabbed hold of her hand and gently tugged her back into her chair. "I'm sorry. It's not a stupid idea. It's a great idea. I would love if you stayed and had dinner with me." He smiled up at her. "My treat—to make up for any undue pain and suffering I might have caused you over that old Barbie doll of yours."

She planted a hand on her hip and sniffed. "She *wasn't* old. She was Superstar Barbie. For your information, she wore earrings and even had a diamond ring on her finger. I was the envy of all my friends."

"Ah, a fine doll, she was," he agreed, lifting his drink in a toasting gesture. "How about I buy you a glass of wine and we can conduct our own personal wake if you'd like?"

Her gaze dropped to the table as she thought about it. Then she slowly met his eyes and sent him a sexy grin that nearly had him sloshing his beer in his lap. "Now how could I refuse an offer like that?"

He quickly put his beer down and cleared his throat. "Uh, then after we have a bite to eat, we'll head right home and check on Brad."

"Absolutely," she said with a nod. "Sounds like a solid plan. After we eat, we'll head straight home."

Walt smiled, but she had agreed to go straight home with more enthusiasm than he would have liked. She obviously wasn't interested in hanging around, getting to know one another better, and repeating—and maybe getting right?—that near-kiss from yesterday. That spark of interest he thought he saw in her eyes must have been confusion, a feeling he could relate to well. Thoughts like those shouldn't be entering his mind anyway. He's definitely lost it. He better tell Kendall to bring him plenty of coffee with dinner. Wine and relaxed inhibitions would only get him into trouble tonight. And trouble where his friend's sister was concerned seemed to be the one place he was heading.

Chapter Seven

Georgie took the last forkful of her white chocolate cheesecake and let out a satisfied sigh. She and Walt were only supposed to have a light bite to eat, but he had eventually strong-armed her into sharing a large unhealthy platter of fried shrimp and clams since Brad wasn't around. Before she knew it, dessert and coffee were placed before her too. Not that she put up much of a fight about it. A little extra caloric intake along with being in Walt's company for the evening certainly hadn't been a hardship to endure.

Walt had even made her laugh out loud at some of the stories he'd told about Brad when they were growing up. She had no idea he and Brad used to go fishing when they were young—or that Brad had fallen off the dock so many times her parents had suggested he just attach the bait to his belt. It was nice to know she wasn't the only balance-challenged member of the family.

She shoved the empty dessert plate to the side with finality. "I shouldn't have eaten all that," she told him, patting her stomach.

Walt took the last bite of his own dessert and grinned. "Sure you should have. It's not going to hurt to indulge in something you know is bad for you once in a while. Especially tonight being such a special occasion and all."

She cocked an eyebrow at him. "A special occasion?"

"Yep, we're celebrating a night of firsts."

Her lips twitched but she managed to keep a straight face. "And what 'first' would that be?"

"Tonight is the first night we've been in each other's company for over an hour and haven't argued."

"Really? Well, the night's not over. I'm laying odds you could still muck things up."

He chuckled. "You know, that's what I like about you, Georgie. You don't hold back from saying what you really feel. You're refreshing to be around."

Georgie didn't want to admit it, but Walt was refreshing to be around too. He was funny and charming and made her forget all about the fact that she wasn't actually on a date. This was the first time since she'd moved back home that she'd been able to relax and have a good time with someone of the opposite sex without any interference from her brother. Something she'd wanted since she'd come home from college. How odd to finally get that from Walt—a person she didn't think would ever treat her as someone other than Brad's little sister.

Walt startled her from her thoughts by reaching out and covering her hand with his. "Hey, you look like you just went a million miles away from me. Did I say something wrong?"

She looked down at their joined hands and swallowed hard. Yes. No. Maybe. She honestly didn't know. The only thing she *did* know was that she felt that familiar fluttering in her stomach as soon as Walt touched her. Then her throat felt tight.

"Uh, I guess I'm just not used to getting compliments," she said with a shrug, pulling her hand away. "My standard MO lately seems to be acquiring lectures—you know, from you, Brad, Al. Even Mrs. Barkat from the pharmacy told me I slouch too much when I'm working at the computer and that I should cut my hair. She doesn't think the length looks professional enough."

"What? Not professional enough? Mrs. Barkat is like . . . a hundred years old. What the heck does she know about professional hairstyles?"

Georgie smiled at his indignant outburst. "Mrs. Barkat is not a hundred years old." Although the woman looked pretty darn close. "She's sixty-two and owned that salon down the street from the pharmacy for over thirty years. So, yes, I think she knows a little something about trends and hairstyles."

"Well, as your boss, I'm telling you not to listen to her. You're professional enough the way you are. *More* than professional. You're perfect. And what are you talking about not being used to compliments? Your idea about the diabetes expo was awesome, and I told you that. What other way can I show you how much I appreciate your idea?"

Kissing me the way you wanted to the other day would be one suggestion, she thought, but she clamped down on her tongue to keep that notion from spewing forth.

Uh-oh. She didn't want to analyze why that thought had popped in her head. *Bad, Georgie, bad.* She shouldn't be lusting after him like that. It was one thing to admire Walt's charm—and body—from afar, and quite another to act on it. She was in dangerous territory. One nice dinner together didn't constitute anything deeper than simple friendship. No matter how kind and attractive she happened to find him.

"Well, well, doesn't this look cozy?"

Georgie blinked up and saw Dee standing next to their table with a satisfied smirk, obviously coming to the wrong conclusion that she and Walt were on a date and maybe even "an item" already.

"This isn't what it looks like!" Georgie exclaimed. Walt's eyebrows shot up, and she blushed. She didn't mean to raise her voice, but Walt had no idea what a hard time they would endure if Dee thought there was anything really going on. People would read too much into it.

"Easy there, hon," Dee said, grinning and squeezing Georgie's shoulder. "I didn't say it looked like anything, except . . . cozy."

"Oh, don't give me your semantics. We both know what you meant. You think Walt and I are on a date. Believe me, this is *not* a date. Right, Walt?"

Walt didn't respond. With a glimmer in his eyes, he simply lifted his coffee cup and took a long sip.

Great. Now was not the time for Walt to be cute. Little did he know that action alone was adding fuel to Dee's gossip fire. He wouldn't be taking this misunderstanding so lightly if he knew what an unusual talent she had of broadcasting news around town. Her mouth practically had its own call letters.

Georgie turned to Dee again. "See? Walt's so shocked, he can't even answer. Brad was here with us, but then he didn't feel well, so Walt and I decided to stay and grab a quick bite to eat. Uh, then you walked in, and, well, here we all are."

Dee peered at the remnants on the table and nodded knowingly. "Hmm. Just a quick bite to eat, eh? I guess you decided to grab a *quick* dinner, a couple of *quick* cheesecakes, and *quickly* linger over a cup of coffee too?"

Walt chuckled. "Busted. But actually, all that was my idea. Georgie wanted to rush back home early tonight. I'm sure she's expecting a call from one of her many would-be suitors. I had to practically chain her to the chair to have her stay here and eat with me."

Georgie sighed in relief. Walt's explanation should squash any funny ideas Dee had about the two of them. She didn't need her friend—or anyone else in town—giving her a hard time about Walt when Georgie wasn't even sure what was going on with him herself.

"Georgie's been a real sport about staying here with me. As you can see I have a rather large appetite," he added.

"Walt has a rather large appetite, Georgie. My, my, isn't that interesting to know?" Dee's eyes shimmered with laughter. "Are you two at least having a good time?"

"Peachy. Until you showed up," Georgie muttered. "What are you doing here anyway, aside from harassing me? Don't you have a diaper to change or a husband waiting for you at home?"

"Actually, I have a hubby waiting for me right over there." Dee raised both arms and waved wildly toward the row of barstools in the back corner of the bar. Her husband, Brody, picked up his pint of beer and saluted them with it—his version of hello. He and Dee never got out that much, even before they had a baby. Unlike Dee, Brody was socially shy and never really felt comfortable getting out and meeting new people. Brody probably saw newcomer Walt and headed straight for the bar.

"All this dating talk of yours made Brody and I realize that we were overdue for a night on the town too," Dee said, beaming at her husband. "So we got a babysitter and decided to have a date night of our own."

Wonderful, Georgie thought. Now even married-with-children people had a better social life and went on more dates than she did.

"Would you two like to join us?" Walt asked.

Dee shook her head. "No, thanks. This is strictly a night for the two of us, but hey, maybe we could all go on a double date sometime," she said with a wink.

"That's real cute, Dee. If you don't watch it, I'll get my so-called boyfriend here to fire you."

Dee just laughed and sashayed back toward the bar.

Georgie felt hot all over with humiliation. Dee's teasing about her dating life made her feel foolish and desperate, which to her dismay was exactly what she was. But Walt didn't need to know that. "Sorry about that. Dee's in rare form tonight."

"Not a problem. What are friends for but to embarrass you in front of other people?"

Georgie couldn't hold back a grin on that one. "Yeah, I guess that's true. Dee is the number one person I complain to about my social life around here. Seeing me on what looks like a date probably sent her imagination into overdrive. I know she doesn't mean any harm. She's just giddy because she's out of the house herself."

Walt nodded thoughtfully. "Yeah, I haven't gotten out in a while either. But you know what? I had a good time tonight, Georgie. A really good time. Thanks," he said, treating her to a muscle-melting grin.

Oh, my, he has a nice smile. She felt herself slipping under the roguish glint in his eyes and quickly had to clear her throat. "Um, why has it been a while since you've been out? You don't have the excuse of having an interfering sibling like I do. Wasn't there anyone special back in Philadelphia?"

Walt's good humor faded. He looked away and didn't answer right off the bat. "Yeah. There was someone." He paused again. "An ex-fiancée."

Ex-fiancée? Brad never mentioned that Walt had been

engaged. The news startled her, and she bolted upright. She wasn't sure how she had expected him to respond to her question, but it hadn't been with the ex-fiancée bomb.

"I . . . see," she said slowly. "Well, if you don't mind me asking—"

"Oh, come on, Georgie. Give me a break here. Let's just enjoy the rest of the evening without you prying into my love life."

Georgie heard the bitterness in his voice, but for some reason pressed on anyway. "You just said you liked the fact that I don't hold back what I want to say. You said it was refreshing. Well, I'm not holding back again. Besides, you can't argue with me now. You'll ruin our night of firsts."

He gave her a long look before relaxing his features a bit and giving into a sigh. "Okay, you win. Ask away. What do you want to know?"

She sat back and crossed her legs. She admired his forthrightness, and it pleased her to have him so readily open up. Most men shut down when she asked them any personal questions. Even her own brother never shared his personal feelings. Yet, here was Walt willing to answer her every whim; another thing that made him so likable to her. Unfortunately.

Georgie knew exactly what she wanted to ask. She bit her lip, trying to come up with a delicate phrasing but quickly gave up and decided to go with her impetuous side. "Well, *fiancée* means you asked someone to actually spend the rest of your life with you, you know what I mean? That's pretty serious. So I don't understand. How could two people who were so committed to one another suddenly break up and decide it was all a mistake?"

Walt blew out another sigh and shrugged. "I don't know. We were together a long time. I think that translated to us as thinking we loved each other. Kiera really didn't like the fact that I was giving up my corporate title, nor did she have any interest in moving here with me. So she made sure she found someone else, then broke off our engagement."

"Oh, she sounds like a fast operator."

"Not really. She didn't have to look far. My friend, Chad, apparently didn't think twice before becoming the new man in her life even though she and I were still engaged."

Georgie flinched, horrified that Walt seemed so calm about the whole situation. "Ouch. That doesn't sound like such a friend to me."

"Yeah. Tell me about it. I think that's why my friendship with your brother means so much to me. He would have never done something like that. He's really a solid guy. I know he's been giving you a hard time, Georgie, but it's only because he worries about you. You're lucky to have someone so loyal like that in your life."

Her shoulders slumped as she thought about Walt's statement. She knew she was lucky to have such a great brother. With her parents gone, she would always have someone looking out for her, caring about her. But weren't there limits to how stifling love could be?

Walt let out a laugh. "You don't look as though you feel very lucky."

She blinked up at him. "Oh, no, I know I'm lucky. Really. It's just that Mom and Dad always watched over me because I was the baby in the family, and, well, now Brad has been treating me as though I haven't shed the infant clothes. I think I need a little break from all this *love* I've been given. A little breathing room."

"Oh?" Walt picked up his coffee and casually took another sip. "What do you mean by breathing room?"

"Well, I want to be free to do what I want. See who I want

to see. At this point in my life I'm not interested in marriage, or dating someone who's 'good for me' as Brad would say. I just want to have a little fun. You know, maybe have a fling or something."

Walt's expression suddenly sobered. "A fling? You want a *fling*?"

Walt's tone stirred up her defensiveness. She already knew where this conversation was headed, and he obviously didn't approve. Maybe "fling" wasn't the best noun choice, but just the thought of forming any serious attachment made her stomach muscles tense.

"Yeah. That's right." She thrust her chin up and looked him square in the eye. "A fling. What do you think about that?"

He didn't answer right away. His jaw clenched as he took out his wallet and tossed a handful of twenties on the table. "I think we should go before I say something that'll spoil this evening. That's what I think." He stood and, without sparing her another glance, stormed toward the front door.

Georgie snatched up her purse and waved good-bye across the restaurant to Kendall and Dee as she scurried after him. "Wait!" she called once she got outside, but he continued to stomp out into the parking lot, heading straight for his car. "Wait! I knew it. I knew you'd think like Brad. But you don't understand."

Walt finally stopped beside his black SUV and whipped around, the expression on his face looking stonier than Mount Rushmore. "Oh, I understand all right. I understand perfectly. You want a no-strings-attached relationship instead of trying to find a nice man to get married and have babies with. Well, let me tell you this: women like *you* aren't supposed to want *flings*. It's wrong. It's not supposed to be in your nature. So just—" He looked up at the night sky and raked his hands through his spiky hair. "Good Lord, I can't believe I'm even having a conversation like this with you! Just what kind of woman are you?"

She drew herself up straight. "I'm a perfectly normal modern woman. Welcome to the new millennium. A simple fling is all I'm looking for at this point in my life. That's nothing to be ashamed of."

"Oh, is that right?"

Walt took a menacing step toward her, his face suddenly inches from hers. She felt her breath being sucked from her lungs as she looked up and saw his eyes lit with a frightening combination of anger and frustration and . . . desire.

He put his arms around her and pulled her to his chest. "Well, all right," he said, low and husky. "If you're looking for a fling, then maybe you should go and have yourself one."

Before her mind could wrap around what was happening, his mouth came down on hers. And it was bliss. Her purse slipped through her hands and she went limp, allowing her body to melt into his. His chest was hard and warm and felt so good against the contrast of the cool evening night surrounding them. She had wanted to kiss him like this, wanted to know what it would be like, but never in a million years had she thought kissing Walt Somers would be this good.

She smelled the piney scent of his cologne and felt the beating of his heart. She slid her arms around his neck and played with the ends of his fine hair as she explored more of his mouth, enjoying its unique taste and the softness of his lips. Then suddenly Walt jerked his head back, holding her at arm's length.

"Wow," he murmured. He dropped his arms and stepped away from her so fast she felt as if a QUARANTINED sign popped up over her head.

She swallowed her hurt and tried to keep her expression

calm. "Um, is that a 'Wow, that kiss was really nice?' or a 'Wow, that kiss was really awful?' "

His shoulders relaxed a bit and a dry smile kicked the corners of his mouth. "Sorry. It was definitely a 'Wow, that kiss was really incredible, and if I hadn't pulled back we would've been two seconds away from someone calling the cops on us.' "

Her eyes widened. She had no idea she had that kind of effect on him. Or could have that effect on any man. But the discomfort in his tone caught her attention. Even if he enjoyed their kiss as much as she did, he obviously still thought it was a mistake. "I feel like there's a 'but' about to follow that statement."

"Yeah, well, there is." He looked down, staring at the tips of his light tan bucks. "Georgie, I've wanted to kiss you ever since you first accused me of stealing those stupid condoms in my own store, and believe me, there's nothing I'd rather do than continue where we left off, but it's just not going to happen."

She blinked. "It's not?"

"No, it's not. I don't know what I was thinking, but I was wrong to say what I did just then when I kissed you, because I don't want a *fling,* as you so boldly put it. And even if I did, I sure as hell wouldn't want to have a fling with my best friend's sister. I'm sorry, but that's not what a real friend would do. I owe Brad that much."

Georgie sagged against his SUV, partly because of shock from Walt's answer and partly because her bearings hadn't straightened out from that kiss yet. Walt didn't want to kiss her anymore because of her brother. She almost laughed, despite her desire not to. Brad wasn't even in a five-mile radius and somehow he was still managing to ruin her love life.

"I felt a connection with you, Georgie. I know you felt it too. So if you're interested in exploring that—like normal people do—and maybe seeing where this relationship takes us, then . . ."

"No," she blurted.

Walt's eyes narrowed and his lips formed two tight lines. "No? That's all you have to say? No explanation?"

Why did this have to be complicated? Yes, she was attracted to Walt. She felt something there, but she didn't want to be in any kind of relationship. She had tried in the past while she was in college with Matt Mandel—until he had left town and her behind. There were scars on her heart that hadn't healed yet to prove it. She couldn't deal with that kind of stuff anymore. Things were better when there wasn't any attachment involved. Why couldn't Walt just accept that? She was offering him what would be an ideal situation for any man.

"What are you afraid of, Georgie?"

Folding her arms, she glanced away. "Nothing," she said briskly. She didn't want to talk about this anymore. She didn't like the way he was looking at her either, as if he could see right through her. It was unnerving.

The restaurant doors suddenly flew open, and Kendall came running out. Once she spotted them, she rushed over. "Oh, I'm so glad I caught you guys," she said, breathing hard and fast. "Georgie, Brad just called. He wants you home right away."

Georgie threw her hands in the air. "Oh, great. It's not even nine o'clock. Now he's setting a curfew on me too?"

Kendall shook her head. "I don't think so, hon. He said there's a bunch of reporters at your door. They're asking for you. Do you think it could involve the date contest?"

Georgie and Walt exchanged stunned looks. "I—I don't

know," she stammered. "I—I have to get home and find out."
She blindly reached down, picked up her purse, and started
to turn away, but Walt seized her wrist.

"I'll drive," he said gruffly. "We'll come back for your car
later."

Georgie saw the no-nonsense expression on his face and
decided now was not the time to argue about her "independence." Besides, between the kiss they'd shared and Kendall's
news, she really wasn't in any condition to drive.

She nodded and climbed in his truck, too worried about
Brad's reaction to the date contest to think about Walt's lips
anymore.

Well, *almost* too worried to think about Walt's lips anymore.

Chapter Eight

Walt held on to Georgie's arm and led her up the path to the condo. Normally, she would have shrugged off his touch, making sure to emphasize that she was quite capable of handling the situation by herself, but something held her back. Instead, she leaned on him, giving in to the comfort he was trying to give her, and it felt surprisingly good. She was glad Walt was there with her. Between the flashes going off and the microphones being shoved in her face, she didn't know how she'd have managed to make it to her front door. As soon as they did, her brother swung open the door. She prayed he would be happy about winning.

More flashes went off. Walt's arm was suddenly around her, and she heard a reporter yell, "Miss Mayer, what was your first reaction when you heard the news?"

Georgie held a hand up to her eyes. The lights they kept throwing in her face appeared like a second sun. She tried to blink away the effects and lost her balance, ending up with her chin in Walt's chest. "Uh . . . well, I guess you could say—"

"No comment," Walt growled and pushed her none too

lightly through the doorway. She stumbled in, and Brad slammed the door behind them.

She could tell Brad was not happy about winning the contest. Air was coming through her brother's nose in short snorty puffs, like a rottweiler picking up the scent of raw meat. Although she was still blinded, she took a weird sort of comfort to learn that her hearing was pitch perfect.

"What the hell, Georgie?" Brad finally cried. "I mean . . . *What the hell?*"

She blinked, allowing her eyes to focus in the normal light, then winced when she could finally see him. The rottweiler image she'd imagined wasn't that far off. In fact, he looked ready to tear her limbs apart at any second.

With his teeth.

She cleared her throat and held up her index finger. "I can explain everything." *I hope.*

"Can we have a word in private?" he asked Walt.

Walt shrugged and took a step toward the bedroom, but Georgie grabbed hold of his arm. "No, it's okay. I think Walt should stay." *As a witness to my attempted murder at the very least.*

"Fine," Brad muttered. "But honestly, what were you thinking, entering that contest, Georgie? Do you know what kind of reputation a guy like Clay Hayes has?"

She opened her mouth, then promptly closed it. One, she wasn't aware of any reputation that Clay Hayes had, and two, why would he be worried about Clay Hayes' reputation if he won a date with Rae Roberts?

Brad whirled around and began pacing the room. "And now you've gone and gotten yourself a date with that guy. You really did it this time. Oh, man, and I thought Tim Clark was bad, but now this."

"Wait a minute," she said, slamming her hands on her hips.

"What was the matter with Tim Clark?" Walt poked her in the back, and she remembered the more important matter at hand. "Oh. I mean . . . did you say I have a date with Clay Hayes?"

"Yeah, Georgie, what do you think I'm so upset about?"

She suddenly felt lightheaded. What was going on? She took a deep breath and began again. "All right. There has to be some mistake. I didn't enter that contest."

Brad stopped pacing and looked at her. His face relaxed a millimeter. "You didn't?"

"She couldn't have entered," Walt chimed in. "She promised me she was only entering you."

Brad's eyes widened to regulation golf ball size, and he thwacked her on the shoulder. "Enter me? You entered *me* in that date contest! What am I going to do on a date with Clay Hayes?"

Georgie shot Walt a thanks-a-lot look then raised her voice over Brad's swearing. "Oh, chill out, will you? Your date isn't supposed to be with Clay Hayes. It's supposed to be with Rae Roberts. But you can forget all about that, because you didn't win."

Oh, my gosh. It hit her then, like an elbow in the back of the head. Brad didn't win. Brad didn't win the date contest. *She* won the date contest.

"Well, thank God I didn't win. But what's worse," Brad said, emphasizing each word with a poke in the air toward Walt, "is that you knew about this whole thing. You should have told me she was up to something like this."

In an instant, all thoughts of her winning the date contest flew from her mind, and she rounded on Brad. "He should have told you?"

Walt looked uneasy, shifting his gaze between her and her brother. "Yeah, well, maybe I should have mentioned what she had in mind to you, but I honestly didn't think anything would come of it."

"See?" Brad said, turning away from her. "This is what I'm talking about. This is exactly why she needs twenty-four-hour surveillance."

"Oh, come on, Brad," Walt said, not masking a chuckle at the ridiculousness of his statement. "Do you really think Georgie needs to be treated as one of your suspects to be monitored twenty-four seven?"

"Yes. As a matter of fact, I do."

Georgie had heard enough. Her lips tightened as she waved both arms in the air to get their attention. "Um, hello? The suspect is present and accounted for, so stop talking about me like I'm not here. And I don't need to be watched and hawked over twenty-four seven. I was just trying to put a little fun in your life, Brad. Who knows? Maybe you would have cracked a smile for once and had a good time."

Brad stared at her, looking all outraged and offended, as if wanting him to be happy was a million times worse than the Alcatraz kind of living he'd been putting her through lately. "If you must know, there have been things on my mind," he said tightly. "So excuse me if I haven't been contributing to this sudden smile quota you've imposed on the house. But if you were that concerned about my laugh muscles, comedy club tickets might have been a better alternative."

She shrugged. "Yeah, well, hindsight and all that."

"I don't understand how Georgie's name could have been entered then. How could she have won?" Walt asked.

Georgie didn't understand it either, but computers and technology weren't infallible. With the way her luck had been heading lately, she should have at least expected something crazy like this. "Look, I don't know how the mix-up happened, but the fact is it happened. So we're all just going to have to accept it and move on."

"Oh no, we're not," Brad said, shaking his head. "You're going to march out there and tell the media that it's all a big crazy mistake and to go home and forget the whole thing."

She blinked, surprised at how highhanded her brother sounded, even for him. This whole situation was confusing, and she didn't mean to upset him, but that didn't mean he could treat her like an idiot and embarrass her in front of Walt.

"Just stop it! Stop ordering me around!" Georgie raised her hand to her pounding forehead. What a mess. She felt one step away from her head snapping off and deserting her body for good. She pressed her eyes shut and tried to think.

What should she do? What did she want?

She wanted Brad to stop telling her what to do, that's what she wanted. She wanted freedom to live her own life. She wanted to date whom she wanted. She wanted independence. She . . .

She wanted to stop thinking about Walt's lips on hers.

There was only one thing left to do about all that. "I'm going on that date," she announced, ignoring their shocked faces. "End of discussion."

"But you can't," Brad said, still looking dazed. "What's the point? Nothing will come of it. You can't have a relationship with someone like him. And you might even get hurt."

"I won't get hurt. Honest. I want to do this." She felt Walt's gaze on her, but she didn't dare look at him to gauge his reaction. A little part of her was curious to know, though. He had said he had felt a connection with her. Now she had probably gone and hurt his feelings by saying she'd go out with another man. But it was for the best.

"You know, it might be good publicity for the diabetes expo," Walt finally said.

Publicity? She swung her head in his direction. Walt was thinking about publicity? She couldn't help feeling miffed at this sudden turnaround in attitude. She thought he'd at least fight for her a little more instead of throwing her on a date with another man so soon.

"Yeah, the diabetes expo," she mimicked, trying to sound upbeat and failing miserably. "Right. I guess some attention would come to it."

"Hey," Brad cut in, eyes aimed like daggers at Walt, "just whose side are you on?"

Walt raised his palms up in surrender. "I'm not trying to be on anyone's side. Clay Hayes is harmless. So what's the problem in capitalizing on that? I'm just trying to be rational here."

"Oh, yeah? Well, go be rational with someone else's sister."

"Enough!" She snapped a little louder than she'd wanted, but she couldn't help it. If she didn't snap, she'd cry. And she wasn't about to show Walt that *her* feelings were the ones that were hurt.

"I'm going to go freshen up and give a statement to the press out there," she announced, thrusting her chin up for effect. "Please, I would appreciate it if you didn't do anything to embarrass me further."

She was met by silence. Taking that as an acquiescence she marched to her room, hoping once again she'd taken hold of her life and made the right decision—and that maybe by going on that date, she'd forget all about Walt's kiss.

Brad sank onto the sofa with his head in hands. "Do you see what it's like with her?"

Walt nodded, gritting his teeth in frustration. Oh, he saw what it was like living with Georgie all right. And she was driving him one short block away from the looney bin.

Had he really said that he thought her winning that date would be good for business?

Business? He almost laughed out loud. Ever since he'd kissed her, business was the furthest thing from his mind.

There was something more than mere attraction going on between them. Something even more than chemistry. He'd never felt a spark like that toward anyone before. Not even toward his ex-fiancée. He didn't know what, but whatever it was Georgie was sure afraid to face it. Maybe he was afraid to face it too, and that's why he had said what he did.

"She's impossible to reason with," Brad said, breaking out of his thoughts. "And because of that she now assumes I'm the worst brother on the planet."

"Don't sweat it. You're a good brother. Georgie knows deep down inside you're just looking out for her."

Brad rolled his eyes. "Gee, I explode on her and practically threaten to handcuff her to the house. Yeah, that really conveys I'm looking out for her best interests."

Walt couldn't resist a grin. "A little extreme for some, but yes. In your defense, Georgie does seem to get herself into more trouble than the average woman."

"So you don't think I said anything that was crazy?"

Walt gave him a noncommittal shrug. Between him and Georgie it was really too close to call who was more crazy. He cleared his throat and went for a more diplomatic response. "Uh, as her brother, you had every right to say what you did and to be worried."

"You've got that right," Brad said with a nod. "And now she's got herself involved with some actor. No thanks to *you*."

"Me?" Walt blinked. Did he exude an "easy target" aura? Both Brad and Georgie seemed to get an unusual amount of satisfaction by pinning the blame for their problems on him. Maybe he should rethink moving in with his uncle, for more reasons than that. "Oh, come on, Brad. You know if I had sided with you, she would have come to the same decision, only ten times faster."

"Yeah, you're probably right." Brad shook his head and let out a hard sigh. "I give up. Maybe I should just stop trying to protect her and let her live her life the way she wants. I should take a Vegas-like attitude—whatever happens . . . happens. You know, butt out of her life."

"Well, I suppose that's the right thing to do," he said, grudgingly.

Brad looked thoughtful for a minute. "Yeah, I could butt out of her life, but . . . but that doesn't mean *you* have to butt out of her life."

Those familiar warning bells went off in Walt's head again as he heard the keenness in Brad's tone. He obviously needed to find a new best friend. "Hold on, I don't like the sound—"

"Yeah," Brad said, a slow grin spreading across his mouth. "You can make sure Georgie doesn't get hurt for me."

"Hey, I thought we already went over this. And we already decided it was a bad idea."

"I know what we agreed, but look." Brad stood and walked over to the coffee table, on which sat a picture of Clay Hayes with a full-toothed grin. He picked it up and waved it in front of Walt's face. "Look at this guy. Do you know what kind of reputation he has?"

Walt didn't know, but he had his suspicions. Just the thought of Georgie and Clay Hayes alone together made his fists clench. He looked away. There was no way he could allow her to go out with some hotshot clown like Clay Hayes—no matter what he'd said about publicity for the pharmacy.

How did he get involved in this whole mess?

When Walt had decided to move back to town, he thought

it'd be nice to be with his family and true friends again. He thought he'd be gaining some stability in his life. But noooo. Instead, his life gets handed a five foot five red-haired walking complication. A complication he felt a totally stupid and inappropriate need to protect that went beyond any friendship with her brother.

"Okay. I'll do it," he told Brad.

"You will? You'd do that?"

"Yeah. I see now what you've been going through. You're right. Georgie is . . . special. And I don't want to see her hurt any more than you do. With me around, Clay Hayes isn't going to think that she's another townie woman he can just love and leave. She deserves more. Much more. Uh, you know, like you said."

"All right," Brad said, folding his arms and cocking his head to the side. "What's going on here?"

"Nothing." He heard the petulant strain in his voice and immediately tried to lighten his tone. "I realized you were right about Georgie. That's all. I mean, what are friends for?"

Brad stared him down for a moment, then he shook his head and chuckled. "Hey, man, I'm sorry for getting all weird on you there. It's just for a moment, I thought . . . never mind. I owe you for doing this for me. At least now I can relax knowing she's in your good hands."

Walt's mouth went dry thinking of Georgie—and his own good hands on her. No, not good. Wrong. His hands weren't going to be anywhere near Georgie. She had made that perfectly clear to him after he'd kissed her. "Yeah. Well. No problem." He averted his eyes and jerked his thumb behind him. "I'll go alert the media out there that Georgie's going to make a statement. I'll try to get a little more information about the date too."

Brad gave him a thumbs-up. "Good thinking. You're a great help."

Help. Right. He was being helpful. He tried to smile, but when it didn't happen he ducked outside before Brad offered any more appreciative comments. Walt was already doubting his involvement in all this. The things he did for his friend. As he marched over to the media, his mind wandered to Georgie and the desire he saw marked all over her beautiful face after he'd kissed her in the parking lot.

Why had she rejected my offer of a serious relationship?

The question was eating at him even though he told himself to forget it. He should have known better than to think that someone like Georgie could so easily be purged from his thoughts. But he assured himself that his decision to stick to her had nothing to do with his attraction to her. Nope, not at all. After all, he was not going to get in the habit of pursuing a woman who wasn't interested in him.

Unfortunately, he hadn't been in the habit of lying to himself either.

Walt just hoped if Brad ever found out he'd understand.

Chapter Nine

You know, for someone who just won the most coveted date this side of the Mississippi, you sure managed to wake up on the wrong side of the bed this morning."

Georgie shot Dee an evil glare—unfortunately only affirming Dee's statement—then went back to cleaning the counting tray.

Yes, she darn well *was* feeling grouchy today. The worst part was she didn't even know why. She'd just won a dream date with a famous television star. Clay Hayes! Nearly every woman in town was probably green with envy by now. So what the heck was wrong with her?

She had her suspicions. Namely, one Walt Somers.

Walt was getting to her. One minute the man kissed her like she was the only woman on the planet, and then the next minute he was practically throwing her into the arms of another man. True, she had rejected him first, but still. It was a callous thing to do to her, and it bugged her. Which only bugged her more. Gosh, if anyone knew how depressed she was, they'd think she had Fruit Loops for brains.

And maybe they'd be right.

Dee waved a hand in front of Georgie's face. "Yoo-hoo, anybody home?"

"Just me and my Fruit Loops," she muttered.

Dee scrunched her brows together and checked her watch. "You're hungry already?"

"No, no, I was just . . . thinking." Thinking about Walt, who just so happened to have made it plainly clear that he was looking to start a serious relationship with her. Also thinking about why in the world she was so down in the mouth about him quickly moving on with his life after she had told him she wasn't interested.

Checking for and seeing no customers lurking around, Dee pulled up a stool and sat down. "I'll bet. So tell me, were you thinking about your upcoming date with Clay Hayes, or were you thinking about your date last night with Walt?"

"Dee! I told you Walt and I were not on a date last night."

"Okay, okay," she said, holding her palms up. "Sheesh, for someone who didn't go out on a date, you sure are touchy about it."

Georgie reached for more alcohol swabs and began cleaning the mortar and pestles. For the third time this morning. "I'm not touchy about it." *Too much.* "I just wish you'd stop calling it a date."

"But I don't understand. A date with Walt is good. He's a nice guy, you know him, and although he tries his best to hide it for whatever reason, I think Walt is crazy about you. If you're worried that Brad—"

"I'm not worried about what he thinks," she snapped. "Walt and I aren't right for each other. That's all. Besides, he's too much like Brad. We both want different . . . Oh, I just feel . . . Did you know he was engaged?"

Dee's brows rose. "Brad was engaged?"

"No," she said with a sigh. "Walt was engaged."

"Oh. No, I didn't, but I consider that a good sign."

"A good sign? How so?"

"Well, for one thing, Walt knows his feelings. That's rare in a man. And second, he's not afraid of commitment. Also rare in a man."

Georgie lowered her eyes, suddenly feeling queasy and overwhelmed. Walt was the type who looked for commitment in a relationship. But a good thing? No, not for her. For another woman, yes. But not her. She wasn't looking for that. A date with a celebrity who'd only be in town a short while sounded much more her speed. After all, a casual night out was all she'd really been hoping for from the beginning. Nothing serious. No chance for any kind of attachment to form. It would be perfect.

So get yourself together and be happy about it then.

A gruff groan caught their attention. Randall slowly approached from the back room, carrying a large bulky box. He managed to maneuver it through the swinging doors, finally stopping by the coatrack, where he let it drop with a loud thud.

"Hey, what's in this thing?" he asked, taking out a handkerchief from his back pocket and mopping the top of his lip.

Georgie rolled her eyes. *Wouldn't it have been nice to ask that before dropping it to the ground?* "Three glucose monitors, some test strips, and a case of Glucerna," she answered, not hiding the annoyance in her tone.

Randall scratched his head. "Why did you want me to bring it out here? Does Walt want us to put that stuff on the shelf or something?"

"No, I just wanted to keep it separate from our regular stock. Didn't Walt tell you about the Diabetes Health Expo we're having?"

His dark brows pulled together like a giant hairy caterpillar. "Expo? Why are we going to have a diabetes expo?"

"Because of this." Georgie made a sweeping gesture of the store with her hand. "Look how dead we are. We need to do something to perk business up, and poor Al can't be worrying about his store while he's recovering."

Randall sniffed. "That sounds like an awful lot of work for no guarantee of success. I don't think it's such a good idea. Besides, Al wouldn't want you getting his store involved in one of your crazy schemes."

Georgie set a hand on her hip, banking down her resentment toward Randall's condescending attitude. "It really doesn't matter what you think, because Walt thought it was a great idea. Didn't he, Dee?"

Dee gave him a smug grin. "That's right, Randall. We hate to pull rank on you, but Walt wants to proceed with the expo immediately. He already had me call the papers and draw up some flyers to give out. He even told Georgie he's hoping the publicity we'll get from the Clay Hayes contest will draw new customers."

Randall shrugged and walked over to get his coffee mug that was drying by the sink, signaling he was done with hearing about the expo and any further talk of her upcoming date with Clay Hayes. Dee and Georgie exchanged aggravated looks, then Georgie glanced out into the store just in time to see Kendall bounce through the front doors.

"Hi, guys," Kendall chirped, giving them a little wave.

Georgie waved back, noticing how pretty Kendall looked this morning with her brown hair down and curling slightly underneath her chin. She wore a bright red long-sleeved tee—which Georgie could never pull off because of her bright orange hair—and boot-cut blue jeans that were simple yet still trendy. Used to seeing Kendall in her work clothes at the restaurant, Georgie had forgotten her friend's good taste in clothes.

Georgie bounced over to the register. "Hey, Kendall," she said. "What brings you by here? You're not sick or anything, are you?"

Kendall shook her head, sending funky red beaded earrings swaying against her cheek. "Nope. Never felt better. I came by for two reasons. First, I wanted to congratulate you on being the lucky lady who's going out for a night on the town with one super hottie Clay Hayes."

"Yeah. It's . . . it's all very, um, exciting."

Kendall and Dee exchanged frowns. "You don't sound very excited," Kendall commented. "I thought you'd be happy about the news."

"No, I'm happy. Really." *Sort of.* "The funny thing is I didn't even enter myself. I only entered Brad. Yet *I'm* the one who won. Don't you think that's a little weird?"

Kendall looked uneasy for a moment, then she perked up and smiled brightly. "Well, maybe there was a mix-up with the names. I wouldn't worry about it. The outcome is much better this way anyhow. Rae Roberts isn't Brad's type at all. Did you see her on the cover of *People?* If her blouse was any smaller, my six-year-old niece could wear it."

Georgie chuckled. "Something tells me Brad wouldn't have complained if Rae Roberts had shown up on their date wearing that blouse."

"Yeah," Dee agreed. "I think any man could endure that kind of hardship."

Kendall folded her arms and harrumphed. "Well, I still can't see him going on a date with her."

Georgie cocked her head at her friend. Kendall almost sounded jealous, which was just about impossible considering Brad was her next best friend after Georgie—and that

Kendall was less than a year away from marrying the love of her life, Jake Grisbaum.

"Okay, so besides wanting to congratulate me on my suddenly enhanced social calendar, why else did you stop by?" Georgie asked.

Kendall's expression softened, and she began digging into her purse. "Ah, to give you two these." She held out envelopes, and Dee and Georgie each took one.

"Oooh, an engagement party!" Dee squealed. "How fun. Do you need me to bring anything?"

Kendall's face lit up. "Well, actually, I was hoping you'd make that monkey bread of yours. Jake loves that stuff. You have to give me the recipe too." She turned to Georgie with a look of amusement. "I already had these invitations printed up, otherwise I would have one for Walt. So be sure to bring him, okay, Georgie?"

Dee elbowed Georgie. "That's right. You know, you really should bring him. You don't even have to call it a date this time."

Georgie didn't let their joking rile her. Or rather, she didn't *show* that their joking around riled her. They also didn't know she and Walt had kissed, or how much it was obviously affecting her.

The phone rang, but Randall didn't make a move to answer it. Dee stuck her tongue out to his back. The phone continued to ring. Dee hesitated another moment, looking torn between her job and not wanting to miss any of Georgie and Kendall's conversation, but she went over to answer it.

As Dee walked away, Kendall pointed her big, inquiring brown eyes at Georgie. "Oh, are you dating Walt? I didn't know that or else we wouldn't . . . I mean, is he okay with you going out with Clay Hayes?"

Georgie thought about Walt and his enthusiasm over the

possibility of any benefit that her date with Clay Hayes would have on the pharmacy and had to squelch her desire to snort. "Oh, he thinks the whole date idea is just hunky-dory."

Kendall bit her lip. "Oh. Well, I guess that's good. I don't know if Jake would be so easygoing about me going out with a rich and handsome celebrity, even if it is for charity. But I'm so glad you finally found someone. You know, I thought you and Walt looked like you were dating."

"No. Walt and I are not dating. We're not doing . . . anything." Not that she hadn't tried to feel him up in one of her Fruit Loop–type conditions the other night in the parking lot. But that would never happen again. She would make sure of it. "We're not right for one another."

Kendall snorted. "Oh, pish posh. Honestly, Georgie, Walt is the first man I've seen you with who actually has some potential."

Georgie worked up a look of mild surprise, and although she knew where this conversation was heading, she asked anyway. "What do you mean by potential?"

"You know, he looks like a guy who *sticks*."

Georgie swallowed hard. A guy who stuck didn't sound all that great. In fact, it sounded downright frightening. People you love rarely stuck. They always left. She had loved her boyfriend, Matt, but once he graduated from college he didn't want to stay around and wait for her to finish her degree. He had left to go back to his own town, telling her it'd been fun but he didn't want to pursue a long-distance relationship. The pain wasn't as deep as what she went through when she'd lost her parents, but her heart hadn't truly recovered.

She couldn't risk that kind of pain all over again.

"Look, Kendall, I'm not interested in a guy like—"

"I *knew* it."

Georgie drew back and blinked, surprised at Kendall's haughty tone. "Knew what?"

Her face set into a decided pout as if she were about to break the news that Georgie had only two weeks left to live. "You've got intimacy issues," Kendall whispered.

"Thank you, Dr. Phil," she said, rolling her eyes for effect. "But I don't have any issues. I'm not crazy here. In fact, I'm perfectly sane. Probably the only sane one in this store."

More sympathy exuded from Kendall's soft brown eyes. "I didn't say you were crazy, sweetie, I said you have intimacy issues. And don't knock Dr. Phil. I've learned quite a lot watching his show. By the way, chronic defensiveness is the first sign."

Georgie blew out a huff and cast a glance over her shoulder. Dee appeared to be busy explaining something to Randall and pointing to the computer screen. Georgie wasn't fooled. Even though Dee looked preoccupied, Georgie had no doubt she was somehow listening in. Maybe even silently agreeing with everything Kendall had just said.

Did she have intimacy issues?

No, of course not. But she felt a prickle of uneasiness when she realized that answer hadn't come to her right away.

Georgie turned her attention back to Kendall and folded her arms. "And just what makes you think I have intimacy problems? I do enjoy going out on dates, you know—when Brad doesn't mess them up."

"True. But you should take a good hard look at the men you've been dating. I couldn't see you seriously dating any of them for any length of time. In fact, I'm surprised—"

"Look, not everyone wants the kind of relationship that you and Jake have, okay?"

Kendall's eyes rounded, looking hurt, and for a brief

moment Georgie felt guilty for her outburst. But just because Kendall had decided to get married didn't mean that kind of commitment was for everyone. It certainly wasn't in the cards for Georgie. She had the Midas touch when it came to relationships. Only everything she touched didn't turn to gold; it disappeared.

Having heard enough talk about dates, intimacy issues, and Walt Somers, Georgie turned away. Of course, that's when she immediately saw Walt stride into the pharmacy.

Her life was turning into a sitcom.

"Well, well," Kendall drawled, shooting him a saucy smile as he approached. "Speak of the devil."

Georgie's pulse quickened as Walt sauntered up to them He looked like he'd been out and about early this morning. His nose and cheeks were already pink, and the ends of his spiky hair were windblown in all different directions. He wore an untucked brown T-shirt with khaki board shorts and smelled crisp and fresh, as if he'd just doused himself with salt air and sunshine.

"Oh, were you talking about me?" he asked, his deep voice thick with amusement. "I'm flattered. It's kind of nice that there's a buzz about me going on already."

Georgie gritted her teeth. Walt had no right to be so happy and charming today. Not when she was so confused and grouchy—and apparently intimacy-challenged.

She scowled. "Why are you here?"

Walt raised an eyebrow at her tone. Unfortunately, he was still breathtakingly handsome even when he was frowning at her. "I'm here because I partly own the store, remember?"

"I know *that*. I mean, it's your day off. Shouldn't you be taking the opportunity to look for more permanent housing?"

He chuckled, but his eyes were cold. She had to resist the sudden urge to rub her arms to ward off the chill. "Thanks for your concern, Georgie, but I have a realtor out doing that for me. What's the matter? Afraid I might cramp your style when Mr. Movie Star comes to pay you a visit?"

"Not at all. It's just that—"

Kendall loudly cleared her throat. "Um, sorry to interrupt this interesting *moment* you guys are having, but I have to run." She turned her attention to Walt. "I'm so glad you're here, because now I can ask you in person. Wanna come to my engagement party this weekend? I'd love for you to meet Jake. A lot of people from town are invited so it might be a great opportunity for you to get reacquainted with everyone again."

Walt's expression warmed, which had Georgie's jaw tightening. She couldn't help feeling jealous, especially when all he'd done since he'd first looked at Georgie was frown and shoot icicles at her with his eyes. "Thanks. I'll be there," he told her.

Kendall beamed. "Great! Well, I guess I better be off." But before she left, she grabbed Georgie's hand and shyly added, "Tell Brad I really hope he comes." She waved good-bye to Dee and Randall, then made a beeline for the doors.

Georgie waited a few beats, then planted a fist on her hip. "So, tell me, why are you really here on your day off?"

"I was on my way over to visit Al and thought I'd see how the progress was going with the diabetes expo. News sure seems to travel fast around here. I had three people stop me in the parking lot to ask me about your contest win."

"Yeah," she said with a weak laugh. "I guess I'm all the buzz around town now too."

Walt didn't crack a smile. He just kept looking at her, sending a strange tingle through her spine. The smoky way he gazed at her now and the way he'd reacted to her date contest news were in contradiction to one another. She didn't understand what was going on between them, but if she could minimize their time together and treat him in a purely professional manner, their relationship might be able to go back to normal.

"Well, if that's all you want from me . . ." Georgie turned away, hoping to make a clean escape.

"That's not all I want from you."

Georgie's heart stopped at the huskiness in his voice. She forced herself to turn around, giving him a questioning look, but his expression remained bland. "I wanted to go over a few more things with you, if you don't mind." He indicated toward the back storage room and grinned. "Step into my office."

She hesitated, casting a glance at Dee, who was watching the two of them as she would her favorite Clay Hayes soap opera. "Um, all right, but just for a minute. I do have work to do."

"I'm sure Dee and Randall can handle things on their own."

She followed his gaze out into the empty aisles. "Oh. Right. Well, people have been calling in their prescriptions all morning. You never know when they'll come by and pick them up. We could get a crowd at any second."

"Then I'll try to make it quick," he said with a wink. He whirled around without a glance back, obviously expecting she'd follow, which she did, trying not to let her gaze focus too long on his backside.

It's no big deal, she told herself. *Admiring a man's body does not mean you want a relationship with him.*

Walt stopped and opened the door for her. Georgie stepped into the storage room and flipped on the light, allowing herself a good look around at the back room. Walt had certainly done a lot with the space available. Al was a bit of a packrat when it came to filing. But now the boxes of prescriptions, which had to be kept for a minimum of seven years, were tucked away in the attic, neatly labeled. There was even a nice, wide walkway now from the break room to the bathroom. The storage area had never looked so organized.

She had to give Walt some credit. Although he'd only been in the store a short while, he'd thrown himself into bettering the working conditions and trying to turn around the store's marketability. He obviously cared a lot about Al and had pride in the pharmacy, which she couldn't help but admire.

Georgie finally turned around and was surprised to see that Walt had been studying her reaction, a smug smile on his lips. He obviously knew she was impressed with what he'd accomplished so far. "Okay. What did you want to talk about?" she asked.

Walt shifted his footing, letting out a hard sigh before answering. "The other night."

Georgie froze. "The other night?"

"Yeah. Look, I—"

"Forget it," she said, and truly wished he would. She didn't want him reading anything further into their kiss. Probably because then she would be forced to as well.

"A momentary lack of good judgment on my part," she continued, even though her cheeks felt like they would melt off her face. "So don't worry about it. As far as I'm concerned that kiss never happened."

Walt's eyes darkened as they narrowed. "That kiss didn't happen, huh? Look, I'm not going to push you, Georgie, but you seem to have no problem with the thought of going out with Clay Hayes. Yet for some reason I can't even get you to acknowledge that you're attracted to me. I'm getting the feeling you're purposely not giving us a chance."

Walt wouldn't let this conversation go, but she was determined to protect herself at all costs. She crossed her arms, giving herself the needed support to stick to her decision. "You're absolutely right. I'm not giving us a chance because there is no us."

Walt took a large step, closing the gap between them. Without warning, he reached out and gently tucked a strand of her hair behind her ear, letting his fingers lazily trail through the ends of her hair and down the side of her neck. She shivered. "We can work on creating an us," he said softly, leaning his face toward hers.

She nibbled her lip as she gazed up at him, her heart pounding with desire for him to kiss her again. But as tempting as he was and as hard as it was to do, she stepped away from his touch. "I'm not interested," she said, more harshly than she intended.

Walt's hand dropped. He stared her down for almost a full minute before he nodded, the expression on his face clearly showing that he didn't believe her. Well, she never was a very good liar. That's one thing that hadn't changed since they were kids.

"Clay Hayes is a lucky man," he murmured.

She looked away and lightly kicked one of the boxes on the ground near her. Her chest felt tight. In her mind she told herself getting involved with Walt would be problematic— that he would want more from her emotionally than she could give—but her body was obviously telling her something else. He was becoming dangerous to be around. "Look, can we just talk about the diabetes expo now and be done?"

Walt let out a frustrated sigh and pointed to the group of boxes she had just kicked. "Tell Randall he can move those to the pharmacy area. Also, when you get a chance today, you can make a list of what we've received so far in donations and who sent them. Then I'd like to send some thank-you notes before it gets too late. Gather to—"

"I know what to do," she snapped. "I told Randall to move everything to the pharmacy area. He obviously must not have seen these boxes. And I already had plans to make a thank-you list this afternoon. So you didn't need to come here and check up on me. I'm not as incompetent as you think I am."

Blame it on her mental Fruit Loops or just being in Walt's presence for too long, but she suddenly felt cornered and defensive. She hated him telling her what to do when she'd been doing things around the pharmacy long before he came to town. The words had flown out before she could stop them. Only snapping at Walt hadn't relieved any of the tension she'd been feeling around him.

Walt's head reeled back. "Hey, easy does it. I never said you were incompetent. I just want to make sure these things get done. I'm not implying you don't know what to do."

"Yes, I believe you were," she said more calmly than she felt. "You obviously think I need to be told how to do everything. Like I wasn't handling things perfectly fine before you and your know-it-all ideas came to town. You're exactly like Brad."

Anger flashed over his face. "Oh, am I? Well, maybe if you didn't go around acting like a flighty brat all the time, I wouldn't feel the need to come in on my day off to remind you how to do your job."

"Message received loud and clear, *boss*. Now you can leave rest assured that you won't have to hold my hand any longer today. Sorry I'm such a burden. Seems like that's all I am to people anymore." To her horror, tears started to fill her eyes.

Walt's anger immediately deflated. His eyes softened, and he instantly reached for her arm. "Georgie, don't be—"

She backed away, afraid her tears would start to spill out once she allowed him to give her even an ounce of comfort. She hated feeling so vulnerable, especially in front of Walt. It made it harder to rely on just herself, to not get attached, to remain independent, and not give in to what her heart really craved.

"No, I'm fine. I'm a big girl." She dabbed the corners of her eyelids with her fingertips, then stuck out her chin to prove that point. "There's obviously nothing left to say. Now, if you'll excuse me, I need to get back to work."

Chapter Ten

Don't you need to get back to work?" Uncle Al asked, glancing at his watch.

Walt refrained from rolling his eyes. Back to work? Ha! Not a chance. He was sorry he'd spent ten minutes of his day off in the pharmacy today. If he hadn't, he wouldn't have gone and upset Georgie so much, they wouldn't have fought, and she wouldn't be thinking what a complete and total jerk he was right at this very moment.

Nice going, big mouth.

Walt could see his uncle's concerned stare from the corner of his eyes, so he quickly stopped beating himself up and pasted on a fake smile. "Nope, it's my day off, so I'm here to visit with you for as long as you want me."

"That's great. It's so nice to have a chat now and again. Keeps my mind from worrying about the store." His uncle leaned forward, shifting the pillows behind his back. He and Walt were sitting companionably outside on Al's deck. The weather was a little crisp to sit out for too long, but Al was dying to get some fresh air since his knee surgery. The doctor had said his uncle was coming along fine and moving about the house with his walker with no problem, but he'd still be out from work for several more months.

Al's face suddenly lit up as he pointed toward the beach. "Hey, look. There's some dolphins."

Walt pretended to follow his uncle's gaze, but his mind remained elsewhere. Nothing could hold his interest now—not a visit with his uncle or dolphins swimming in the morning sunlight. Heck, he wasn't sure if Angelina Jolie in a bikini could hold his attention right now. He couldn't stop thinking about the tears he'd seen in Georgie's eyes.

And, worse, how he had put them there.

"You seem troubled, Walt. Do you miss the city? Are you adjusting to small-town living okay?"

Walt tried to take a deep breath, but his chest felt as if he had a car parked on it. He really wished that the town itself was the source of his problems. "No, I like Maritime City. The people are just as nice as I remember. And business is doing a little better too. I think the diabetes expo will make an even bigger impact."

"Yes. Georgie had a great idea there. I told you she was smart as a whip."

Walt could only grunt in response.

Al looked at him sharply. "I'm afraid I'm not quite up to date with the young person's lingo. Is that grunt code for something? Georgie giving you problems?"

Major problems. With her brother. With the store. With his head. And most of all with his heart. "No, no problems that I can think of."

Al sat back again. "Oh, that's good. Well, tell me, has Georgie met any nice young fellows yet?"

"No," he snapped, crossing his arms over his chest and giving in to his grouchy mood. "In fact, she's gone and won herself a date with that Clay Hayes character. A Hollywood actor! Can you believe that one?"

"Ah, yes," Al said calmly, nodding. "I read that in the paper. Well, that's nice. It's for the town and charity after all."

"Charity my big toe," Walt scoffed. "All that guy is after is a little small town diversion with a pretty redhead who happens to be too stubborn to realize that *she's* the small town diversion."

Raising his eyebrows a clear inch up his forehead, Al cleared his throat. "Oh, I see."

Walt caught the knowing look on his uncle's face and grew defensive. What was the point of admitting how he felt about Georgie? She had obviously put up a six-foot fence around her feelings. He assumed that's why she'd picked that fight with him at the pharmacy. That was her way of dealing with things—lashing out then pushing away.

Well, maybe it was time for him to listen to her and move on.

"No, Uncle. You don't see anything."

"But—"

"There's nothing to see."

"Oh, I s—"

"Don't say it again," he warned.

"If you say so."

"Well, I do."

Several seconds ticked by.

"So, how long have you felt this way about Georgie?" his uncle finally asked.

Walt let out the breath he'd been holding and hung his head in defeat. "I think ever since she accused me of stealing those stupid condoms."

Al made a tsking sound. "Then I'm afraid you've got it bad, my boy. Does Georgie know?"

"Yes. No. Sort of. Well, she knows I'm attracted to her. And she's attracted to me. That's the kicker. But she keeps shutting me out. It doesn't make any sense. Everything is so crazy. She's crazy." *And loyal, and hardworking, and smart, and beautiful, and everything I could want in a woman.*

Al looked at Walt like *he* was the one who was crazy. "Georgie's crazy like a fox I'd say. She's probably just playing hard to get."

Walt wished it were as simple as a woman playing hard to get, but he knew differently. Something more was going on. "No, she's not a game player, not like Kiera was. Georgie is unique. She's a very upfront woman, which is one of the things I really like about her. I think she's got this notion in her head that I'm like her brother, that I don't take her seriously. I *do* take her seriously, but she misinterprets my caring about her as interference. I don't know how to get through to her."

"Well, people besides her brother have been looking out for Georgie for a long time. I think the whole town—including myself and your aunt—took her under their wing because she was so young when her parents died. It's only natural that she'd get tired of the attention and want some space to stand on her own two feet after a while."

"Thanks a lot," he shot back. "You're a big help. So you think I should ignore my feelings and let her enjoy her independence, is that it?"

"Not at all, son. What I'm saying is that Georgie may *think* she knows what she wants, but true feelings are always in the heart, not in the head. Unfortunately the mind is a pretty formidable opponent. Just show her the difference, and you'll be fine."

Walt stared at Al for a few more moments, hoping more aged wisdom would come from his uncle's mouth. When nothing else came forth, Walt made a face. "That's it? That's the best advice you could give me? Am I the only person in this town that can make sense?"

Al picked up the newspaper on the table and swatted Walt with it.

"Ow!" he cried, rubbing the back of his head. "Why did you go and do that?"

"To knock some sense into that thick skull of yours, boy. Listen up. I'm giving you some advice, but obviously you're too dang proud to hear it. If Georgie thinks you're acting like Brad, then for heaven's sake stop acting like a brother. Treat her like she wants to be treated, so she can realize her feelings. Don't just roll over and play dead."

Walt lowered his hand and thought for a minute. "So you're saying I should ignore what she's been telling me and just go after her?"

His uncle crossed his arms with a satisfied smile on his lips. "The man can be taught."

Walt shook his head and chuckled. Obviously Uncle Al was a romantic at heart, but he didn't understand the complications of how a man and woman dealt with one another in this generation, especially when a man had to deal with as big of a complication as Georgie Mayer. But at this point, he had nothing to lose, aside from his friendship with her brother. It was a risk he had to take. Starting right then, Walt was going to show Georgie just how "unbrotherly" his feelings toward her were.

Georgie narrowed her eyes and gazed around the room filled with people. Jake and Kendall's engagement party was jumping. Groups of people huddled together in various spots around the house, mingling and eating and laughing. She wanted to join them but she couldn't let herself relax and enjoy it quite yet. She had business to attend to first. She was determined to help Brad out, whether he wanted it or not.

Jake's tiny rancher was jam-packed, only with very few single women. Two out of the three firefighter platoons had shown up to congratulate him on his engagement to Kendall. Quite a few cops from the police department showed up too. Kendall was beaming all night, but Georgie could tell she was disappointed that Brad wasn't there. He surprisingly decided to put in for some overtime at work at the last minute. He told Georgie that he'd try to swing by at the end of his three to eleven shift, but that news didn't make her or Kendall any happier. Brad seemed to be resorting to hermit status, purposely going out of his way to avoid a good time.

What was going on with him?

Georgie suddenly zeroed in on another potential date candidate for Brad and pulled out a small spiral notepad she'd brought with her. She jotted down the name, then reviewed the page. So far she had a pretty good list going. Eight women in all. Not too shabby, especially in this type of atmosphere. Georgie hated to use her friend's engagement party as a vehicle for acquiring dates for her brother, but the situation was desperate. She had just heard from Dee that Brad had already volunteered to be put on as one of the police escorts Clay Hayes would need when he got into town. Good Lord. Hopefully, Brad wouldn't get the assignment. All she needed was her brother accompanying her on a date. She wasn't sure how much more of his overprotectiveness she could take.

"At it again, are we?"

Georgie jumped even though Walt's question was said soft and sexy in her ear. Where had he snuck up from? She had seen him arrive at the party a little less than an hour ago but had craftily managed to avoid him—up until now, that is.

She snapped her notebook shut and turned around, trying not to let the delicious smell of him distract her. "No, as a matter of fact, *we* are not at it again. *I* am at it again." She shot her hand to her mouth and winced. "Uh . . . I mean, I'm not up to anything. Just standing here, uh, enjoying a lovely party."

He grinned. "Right. I can see that," he said, motioning toward the notebook she had in her hand. "But as Brad's best friend, I think I have to warn him this time."

"Well, as *my* friend, could you at least wait a few weeks before you go and blabber to him about it?"

Walt's expression turned serious, and he dipped his head so he could look directly into her eyes. "I don't know. Are we still friends, Georgie?"

She smiled and allowed herself to get lost in the green-gray depths of his earnest eyes. For only a moment, her heart could afford just one small indulgence. "Yeah. I guess we are."

Walt made a show of wiping imaginary sweat off his forehead.

She chuckled, and her heart felt ten times lighter, knowing that they were still able to enjoy each other's company. The last couple of days since their fight had been rough. She'd missed this, his friendship, being able to laugh with him again.

"Look, Walt, I've been meaning to say this to you but I haven't had the chance. I . . . I want to apologize for overreacting the other day in the pharmacy. I was in a mood, and I took it out on you. I'm so sorry."

"Apology accepted," he said with a solemn nod. "But only if you accept my apology first. I was way out of line too. I shouldn't have called you a flighty brat."

"Thank you."

"I should have called you a conscientious brat instead."

She laughed but punched him on the arm. "Are you mocking me?"

Walt took hold of her fist and flattened her hand against his heart. "Never," he said huskily.

As startling as a needle being pulled off a record player, all joking ended between them in that split second. Red flags waved in front of her eyes, and she suddenly grew wary of his simple touch. She blinked and tried to weakly pull her hand away from his, but he wouldn't let it go. He just kept looking at her, his eyes steady and searching for something she wasn't ready for him to see. Suddenly, she felt as if she were standing in quicksand. And sinking fast.

"Don't," she whispered, tugging her hand again.

Walt tightened his grip, keeping her hand firmly against his chest. "Don't what? Don't look at you? Don't touch you? Don't be your friend? What exactly do you want from me, Georgie?"

"I . . . I . . ." She groaned inwardly. What she wanted and what she was afraid to want seemed to be the same thing. Could she allow herself a little indulgence with Walt and still keep her emotions in check? She didn't think so. She was so afraid to let go and grow attached to someone again. Walt hadn't been in town long. He hadn't even found permanent housing yet. What if he decided to leave and move back to Philadelphia? She had to protect herself.

"Well, well, Georgie," a woman's voice drawled from behind her, "you sure are batting a thousand this month."

Georgie slipped her hand from Walt's grasp, turned around, and saw Vivian Reynolds. Vivian moved to town a few years ago with her husband, a frequent customer of the pharmacy. She was a few years older than Georgie, now divorced, and dating one of Jake's buddies in the fire department. But at the moment she'd seemed to have forgotten that last little tidbit of information, seeing that her attention was solely and inappropriately directed toward Walt.

"Hi, Vivian," Georgie said with a frown. "What do you mean I'm batting a thousand this month?"

Vivian licked her clear-glossed lips, her half-lidded gaze still focused hungrily on Walt. "I just mean, first you win a date with that gorgeous Clay Hayes and now I find you holding hands with this charming specimen of a man. By the way, I don't believe we've met," she said, shifting around Georgie.

Georgie folded her arms, not appreciating the sneaky way Vivian had just inserted herself between her and Walt. "Well, maybe if you shopped in the store more, you'd know that this 'charming specimen of a man' happens to be the new pharmacist."

Vivian cocked a blond penciled eyebrow at Georgie's curt tone, then turned her attention back to Walt. "You don't say. Well, I'm Vivian Reynolds," she told him, holding out her French-manicured hand to Walt, who politely took it with a smile. "I'm sure you'll be seeing me around the store a lot more."

"Oh, and why is that?" Georgie asked with exaggerated innocence. "Did you hear about the sale we're having on foot odor products this month?"

Walt raised his hand to muffle up his chuckle. Vivian shot Georgie an evil scowl. "Well, I can see I'm crossing a heavily guarded line here. Are you and Walt dating?"

Georgie hesitated, feeling the color drain from her face. "Oh, well, no. Walt and I are . . . we're just friends." Yeah. That was a perfectly good description for her and Walt. Friends. Although she found it a little disconcerting that the word almost got stuck on her tongue.

Vivian's mouth curved into a slow seductive smile. "That's very fortunate for me then. Kenny and I broke up a few weeks ago."

"You did?" Georgie could hear the disappointment in her own voice and winced. She hoped Walt and Vivian didn't have as acute hearing.

"Yes, I'm afraid so," Vivian said with a fake sigh. "I guess you can say I'm on the market again." Gazing longingly at Walt, she added, "I bet you haven't gotten out much since you've been in town. I could show you around to all the great hot spots."

"That's very kind of you to offer," Walt said.

Georgie took one look at the charming smile Walt was shooting at Vivian and had the sudden desire to kick Vivian's three-inch heels out from under her. "Well, that's all very interesting to hear, Vivian," she said hastily, grabbing Walt's arm and pulling her with him. "But Walt and I have to discuss something else, er, business. We have to discuss pharmacy business. Top secret stuff. Walt will look you up, I'm sure, though. See ya around."

Georgie continued to pull Walt across the crowded room and out the front door—stopping only briefly to make sure Dee was not witnessing any of this—until they ended up outside on the porch. The evening air was breezy and chilly and thankfully just what she needed to cool herself down in a hurry.

"Just what were you doing back there?" she accused.

Walt blinked, then let out a laugh. "I was going to ask you the same thing. 'Oh, did you hear about our sale on foot odor products?'" He held his stomach and started laughing again. "Oh, come on. That was just plain cruel. Hilarious, but cruel."

Georgie reluctantly gave in to a smile. "Okay. So maybe

that was a teensy weensy bit mean, but she deserved it. Vivian is too much, and I didn't like the way she was looking at you."

"Oh, yeah?" Walt angled his head, still smiling. "You didn't like how she was looking at me?"

"No, I didn't." She swallowed hard, realizing she had just stupidly backed herself into a corner. "But . . . only because . . . well, I didn't want you being selfish and taking any potential dates away from Brad. That's all. I could have added her to my list, you know," she pointedly informed him, waving her notebook in front of his face.

Walt snatched the book out of her hand and tossed it on the ground. "Why, Georgie?" He raised both hands, his fingers raking the air in frustration. "You're so focused on your brother's love life that you're ignoring your own. And mine, by the way. So, tell me. Why are you so intent on finding a woman for Brad?"

"I told you," she said, thrusting her chin up. "I don't want him to worry about me. I can't concentrate on my own love life if he's too busy worrying about mine. He needs a life. I feel like a huge burden to him right now."

"You're not. Brad—"

She held up a hand. "I know. He loves me." She let out a heavy sigh. Frustrated with Brad, with Walt, with Vivian, but mostly with herself. Brad had so much love to give. Someday he was going to make a woman extremely happy— if he ever got out of the slump he was in and found one, that is.

Georgie lowered her eyes and stared at her notebook of names, lying haphazardly on the grass. Maybe her method of finding Brad a woman was a little unconventional, but her brother deserved a little happiness.

Was that so wrong to want that for at least one of them?

She released another breath and a little bit of tension drained from her shoulders. "Look, I don't want to fight with you, Walt."

"All right. Let's get out of here then."

Her eyes widened. "You want to leave? But you haven't even been here an hour yet."

"Ah-ha!" he said triumphantly, pointing his finger at her. "I knew you were avoiding me. So you *did* see me come in."

Her face heated. Thank goodness half the firefighters in town were just a few short yards away, because she had a feeling her cheeks would ignite off her face at any second.

"Well, of course I saw you come in," she said in a huff. "Anyone with an ounce of estrogen in her body saw you walk into the party tonight. I'm sure Vivian had you in her radar as soon as she heard your truck pull up."

Walt grinned, looking like he'd just won Man of the Year. "Come on," he said, taking hold of her hand and leading her down the porch steps.

Georgie followed, too tired to fight with him anymore, but when he opened the door of his truck for her, her heart chickened out and she dug in her heels. "Where are we going?" she demanded.

"You'll see," he said, reaching out and gently running a finger along her cheekbone. "I want to show you something."

She backed away from his truck—and more importantly, from his touch. "Oh, no. I don't think so. I've heard that line before."

Walt cocked his head, letting a sexy little grin slip out. "Georgie, if you're worried that I want to take you somewhere so I can take advantage of you, well, then you'd probably be smart to worry. But as it turns out, I would really like to show you something. It won't take long. In fact, I doubt we'll even be missed."

Georgie bit her lip as she stared at the mischievous glint in Walt's eyes. *Don't go! Don't go!* her mind screamed. He looked far too good tonight in his faded blue jeans. The way his navy V-neck polo dipped just south enough for her to get an eyeful of that sexy little patch of chest hair made a wicked part of her want to reach out and run her finger all along the exposed area of his skin. She swallowed hard. The more time she spent with him, the more he was getting to her.

Going somewhere—anywhere—with Walt Somers had bad idea tattooed all over it. If she were a smart woman, she'd say no thank you, and turn away. What was she doing encouraging a man who had been engaged before and therefore probably still looking for some woman to settle down with?

Walt deserved better than her.

If she were smart, she'd pick up her notebook off the ground, march right back to the party, and have herself a cold drink. Maybe two. That's what a smart woman would do. A smart woman with no interest in getting involved in any type of relationship with a man as dangerous and sexy as Walt. The only thing was . . .

She wasn't very smart.

Chapter Eleven

It wasn't smart picking up and leaving the engagement party with Georgie like that. In fact, Walt was darn positive gossip was already spreading about the two of them at that very moment. But he didn't care. If he didn't steal a moment alone with Georgie now, he wasn't sure when he'd be given another chance—or if he would even have the nerve again.

Walt put his turn signal on and made a left. The destination he had in mind was just a mile ahead now. Georgie stared out the window in silence as he continued to drive. She didn't know it, but every once in a while he would glance over at her, taking in the lovely shape of her profile bathed in the moonlight and stars.

He waited for some reaction or question from her. He knew her well enough to know that her curiosity about where they were going had to be killing her. But she hadn't said much since he'd started the truck, and if Georgie had an inkling of where they were headed she hadn't made it known.

He slowed down and pulled into a long dirt driveway at the corner of the street. When he reached the end, he shut off the engine and turned to her expectantly. "Well, what do you think?" he asked.

Georgie's brows furrowed as she gazed out the windshield. "Um, what do I think about what?"

"This," he said, raising his hand and indicating the yellow rancher in a sweeping gesture. "I close on it Monday."

"You bought a house?" Her interest perked up with each blink of her eye. "*This* house? *Already?*"

Walt chuckled at the shocked look on her face and dangled a pair of keys in front of her eyes. "Technically, it's not mine just yet, but my Uncle Al is good friends with the owner so they gave me the keys early. Come on, I want to show you the inside." He opened his car door and felt a sense of pride as he looked at his soon-to-be investment for the future.

"Oh, so this is it? You're really moving out then?" she asked, following him up the sidewalk.

Hearing the disappointment in her voice, Walt tried not to smile. He knew it. Georgie was going to miss having him around. Good, because he had plans that would put her exactly where he wanted her—living with him. Without her brother.

"Well, that's what one does when one buys his own house," he remarked casually. "I'll start packing up this weekend, so I'm ready to move out by Monday night." He stuck the key in the lock and opened the front door. Weaving her arm through his, he then nudged her stiff body forward. "Hey, don't tell me you're actually going to miss me."

"Miss you?" She laughed, but he could tell it was forced. "This is a dream come true to finally be rid of you. It'll be fantastic not to have your luggage in my room anymore, and now I won't have you drinking up all the coffee on me in the . . ." Her words trailed off as she gazed around the living room space. The stone gas fireplace that had just been put in made an eye-catching focal point to the room, and the bleached hardwood floor shined in the dimmed recess lightning. "Oh, my gosh," she gasped, dropping her arms to her sides. "This is lovely, Walt."

"I thought you'd like it."

She slowly circled the room, stopping at the small bar area to run her fingers along the smooth granite counter. "I would have never guessed all this was in this tiny little rancher."

"It's not that tiny. Plenty big to start a family once I'm married."

Her face fell and her milky white complexion grew even paler. "A family? Aren't you jumping the gun a little thinking about raising a family when you're not even engaged?"

Not engaged yet, he thought.

"Never hurts to think ahead," he said with a shrug. "Did you know this place has three bedrooms and two-and-a-half baths?"

"Hmm . . . I guess that is pretty roomy."

"It is. Perfect if you ever want to spend the night with me." He coughed and cleared his throat. "What I mean is that if you and your brother ever have a fight or anything, there's always room for you here."

Amusement danced in her clear blue eyes. "Uh-huh. Thanks. I'll keep that in mind, considering the number of fights Brad and I seem to have on a weekly basis. But I'm sure you wouldn't want me to interfere with your newfound bachelor pad."

"Hey, you wouldn't interfere at all. Being single isn't all that great anyway. In fact, being a bachelor can be quite . . . lonely." Although having a fiancée had been just as lonely. Even before he'd found out Kiera had been cheating on him, something obviously had been missing from their relationship. Walt had been blinded by her beauty and was satisfied enough with having someone to warm his bed. He had been hurt badly by his parents' divorce, so at the time that was all he'd wanted—to keep her and others at a distance. Like Georgie had wanted to keep him at a distance. Maybe that was why he felt such a kindred spirit toward her. He was fortunate to have broken off his engagement to Kiera before it was too late. Before he'd realized he hadn't had any real feelings for her. The kind of feelings he should have had for the woman he was about to marry.

The kind of feelings he had for Georgie.

He had finally found the something that had been missing from his life. Surely, her brother couldn't hate him for that. Walt supposed he'd always loved Georgie—her impetuousness, her sense of humor, her clumsiness, her loyalty to her brother and to Al. But now he was *in love* with her. And he wanted to spend the rest of his life with her.

Starting right now.

"I don't know," she said wistfully. "Loneliness has its advantages."

Her words jolted him back to reality, and he did a double-take. He wanted to grow closer and Georgie suddenly wanted to talk about how great being alone was. Why had he expected anything different? Leave it to her to make things ten times more difficult for him.

"Wha—what do you mean by that?" he stammered. "What kind of advantages are there to being alone?"

She stared at the hardwood floor for a few seconds, fingering her mother's locket, then she lifted her gaze and shrugged a shoulder. "For one thing you never feel smothered."

"You never feel loved either."

"Same thing." She started to turn away, but he seized her wrist, stopping her. She was lucky her wrist was all he had hold of, because he really wanted to take hold of her shoulders with both hands and shake some sense into her head as well.

"Georgie, I—"

"Love isn't in the cards for everyone," she said quietly.

How could she say that?

He wanted to demand an answer to that, but her baffling statement, her poignant look, the whole situation left him completely speechless.

She pried his fingers off of her wrist, then quickly walked away to take a look at the kitchen. "So you're really staying around? I mean, for good? I guess you must really like this town."

Walt walked up behind her and rested his hands on her shoulders. "I do like this town and a few other things here."

Her body tensed at his touch, but he wasn't about to let her change the subject or get away so easily. Not when all he'd been able to think about since they'd stepped foot in the house was confessing his feelings and touching his lips to hers again.

Georgie turned around, gazing up at him with tentative eyes—as if she knew exactly where his thoughts were heading. Because of that, Walt half expected her to slip away and start chattering about the house again. He would have let her if she had, as much as it would have killed him. There was no use forcing something she wasn't feeling. But she surprised him by reaching her hand around his neck and leaning his head down to hers. He didn't waste any time analyzing her reasons for meeting him halfway. He only wanted to lose himself in the heady spell Georgie had already cast on him. So he quickly cupped her face with his hands and kissed her.

She surprised him again by kissing him back with an

equal vengeance. The softness of her body brushed against his, and he gathered her up against him. He wanted her to know what she did to him, how he made her feel—praying she felt what he felt. The sweet and airy scent of her skin smelled like fresh summer fruit; he couldn't decide if he wanted to just inhale her or take a bite.

He chose to come up for air instead.

"That's one of things I really like about this town too," he said, smiling against her mouth.

She swallowed hard. "Yeah," she said breathlessly. "I—I can see why."

He chuckled, even though he wanted her so much he couldn't see straight. But he wasn't going to rush her. This was new and different for him, and he was going to make sure it was different to her too. Not a fling or something temporary. He wanted to take up permanent residence in her heart.

Just like she had with him.

He leaned his forehead against hers and gazed into her eyes. "I have something else I'd like to show you."

"Oh yeah?" Her lips curved. "What else do you want to show me?" she murmured.

"The sign I made up for the diabetes expo. You're going to love it. It's in the trunk of my car."

"The expo sign?" She blinked then laughed out loud. "After that kiss you're thinking about a sign? Oh, my gosh, Walt, you're driving me crazy!"

Walt grinned as his fingers combed through the loose curls of her long red hair. *Crazy is good,* he thought. Georgie had drove him his fair share of crazy these last few weeks, so it was only right that he inflict a little of the same torture. He considered it a good sign that she was so easily frustrated when it came to him. She might not have said she was in love with him, but crazy was definitely a start. And if she canceled that ridiculous date with Clay Hayes, he'd consider it a fantastic start.

He dropped his arms and forced himself to keep his hands at his sides. "Maybe we should head back," he suggested.

"Back?" She cocked her head, her expression still half dazed. "Back where?"

"To Kendall and Jake's engagement party. People are probably wondering where we went off to."

Georgie sprang backward, alarm registering on her face. "Oh, jeez, you're right. If Dee saw us leave, we're totally busted. She and Kendall—you don't know them like I do— they're probably planning *our* engagement party as we speak." She let out a nervous laugh. "If you could imagine something as funny as that."

Walt *could* imagine that. But he didn't find it funny at all. Maybe a few weeks ago he would have laughed at the thought of he and Georgie engaged, but not now. Now that was all he wanted. It seemed Georgie did not want the same thing.

Yet.

He extended his hand to lead her out and she took it, entwining her fingers with his. Their hands joined together felt right, but he knew if he so much as mentioned that thought to Georgie, he'd scare her away. For whatever reason, Georgie wanted to avoid serious relationships. Convincing her that they were meant for one another was going to be tricky, but considering how comfortably she left her hand in his, he felt he was heading along the right path.

"So . . . anything delightfully naughty happen when you and Walt disappeared from Kendall and Jake's party the other night?" Dee asked, propping her elbows on the counter and giving Georgie her one hundred percent full attention.

Georgie walked into work not surprised by Dee's keen interest in her love life. After all, she had assumed Dee had seen her leave the engagement party with Walt. So, naturally, Dee would assume that there was something more going on between them than friendship—which there wasn't. There couldn't be. Now the only problem was trying to convey that to her friend before half the town—and especially Brad—heard otherwise.

"So?" Dee prompted eagerly. "You gonna spill the juicy details or what?"

"Oh. Well, let's see . . ." Georgie put on her lab coat and pretended to find Dee's question amusing. "Um, he did hold my hand. Twice."

Walt had kissed her twice too, but Dee didn't need to know that, or that he had talked about marriage and starting a family and . . . Good Lord, she suddenly couldn't breathe. Why, oh, why had Walt mentioned all that stuff to her? Did he want more than friendship? Was he now thinking about getting back together with his fiancée?

Ugh, why was she even thinking about it?

Because she was a mess. That's why. She didn't have Fruit Loops for brains like she'd thought the other day. Nooooo. Her mental status had slithered down a notch.

She was now officially cuckoo for Cocoa Puffs.

And it was all Walt's fault.

Dee made a face. "Walt held your hand? That's *it*? You guys were gone an awfully long time for just some simple hand holding to be going on."

"He only wanted to show me the house he's buying. Nothing sordid or naughty whatsoever."

"I know. That's the problem."

Georgie rolled her eyes. Leave it to Dee to want her soap opera stories to come to life. "Sorry to disappoint you, but

Walt and I are just friends. Good friends." Good friends who had held hands. Good friends who had kissed. No big deal. At least she was trying to convince herself it was no big deal, and that she could treat Walt just like she had any other man she had briefly kissed or held hands with—and continue to keep him at arm's length.

Suddenly a tall older man with a full head of wavy gray hair stepped up to the counter and caught Georgie's attention. She walked over and immediately greeted him.

"What's this about some diabetes thing you're having?" he asked, holding up one of the flyers they had distributed a few weeks ago.

"Oh, we're going to have a diabetes expo set up here in the center of the pharmacy," she answered proudly. "There'll be a pharmacist and a diabetes educator on hand all day to answer questions about the disease, and we'll be giving away some free samples of various products and raffling off a few glucose monitors. Are you interested in setting up an appointment to talk with one of the health care professionals?"

The man thought it over, then nodded. "My wife has diabetes. I know she'd like to come in and get some help with that. Do you have to get your medications here to come to the expo?"

"Not at all," Georgie said, smiling. "The health fair is open to anyone in the community who wants to get educated on the disease."

He dug into his back pocket and pulled out his wallet. Lifting out a crumpled prescription that was folded between his money, he smiled, then held it out to Georgie. "Well, I think I'd like to start coming here to get my prescriptions filled."

"That's wonderful, Mr."—Georgie took the slip of paper and glanced at the name—"Mr. Sheppard. I'll just need your insurance card. Dee over here will need to ask you a few questions so we can put all your information into our computer."

As she handed the prescription over to Dee, Georgie saw Walt enter the store. She couldn't wait to tell him that the expo was already attracting customers and raced down the aisle toward him.

"Guess what?" she prompted, smacking him in the shoulder.

Walt watched her bounce up on tiptoe with amusement. "Let me guess. You've entered Brad in another date contest?"

"Of course not." She laughed, then quickly frowned. "Wait. Is there another date contest?"

"Georgie . . ." he said with a hint of warning.

"I'm kidding! Seriously, I just wanted to tell you that I've already had someone want to transfer their prescriptions to our store and all because of the diabetes expo. We have two clipboards full of appointments for the diabetes educator too. How's that for progress?"

"Hey, that's great. After we see how the expo turns out, we should brainstorm some more ideas. I think if we put our heads together, we might be able to keep this store afloat. We make a good team, you and I."

Georgie beamed. She didn't even have her pharmacist license yet, and Walt was already considering her part of the team. His team. Funny, but she didn't mind the way that sounded at all. It was so easy to think of herself as part of his team when it came to the pharmacy, but when it came to being on his team for anything more . . . her stomach did a backflip.

"Where's Randall?" Walt asked, looking over her head. "I made the new schedule and I wanted to go over it with him before I go to settlement."

"He must be in the break room. Uh . . . you're definitely

moving out today?" She tried to smile and remind herself that distance from Walt would actually be a good thing.

"Got my bags packed and everything." He cocked his head and gave her a thoughtful look. "You know, if you're not busy tonight, you could always swing by my place and keep me company as I unpack. You think you could spare to spend your free time with me?" His question surprised her so she hesitated, and his expectant face suddenly fell. "Oh, sorry. Do you have other plans?" he asked.

Her only plans were watching her brother polish his shoes and gun for work tomorrow. But even if she had other plans, she'd still consider hanging out with Walt a much better option. And a far more dangerous option.

"I'll have dinner waiting, and I should have some furniture for you to sit on by then too," he added.

"You went furniture shopping already too?"

He chuckled. "No, I had some stuff in storage from my place in Philadelphia. The movers should be there by two this afternoon. So what do you say? Actually, I still want to go over some things for the diabetes expo. We can do it while I unpack."

"Well . . ." *Business, Georgie. He just wants to talk business. Don't be such a chicken.* "Okay, I guess I could come over then."

"Great," he said, looking relieved. "I was hoping you'd come."

For a long moment their eyes met, and neither of them said another word. It hit her then how adorable he looked, standing there in his Phillies baseball cap and surfer board shorts, just like how she remembered he'd looked back in high school—only now he had muscular legs. She couldn't help but wonder what he saw when he gazed at her. Did he still see Brad's little sister?

"I'll go give the schedule to Randall now," he said, jerking his thumb behind him. "I'll order a pizza tonight. And wine. I won't *order* the wine, just the pizza. I have some already. We can drink it. The wine, that is." He winced and shook his head. "I'll see you tonight." With that he cut himself off and walked away.

For a second there, Walt almost seemed unsure of himself, and she had to grin. There was definitely a sweetness about him when he lost the highhanded attitude like her brother's. She didn't want to analyze why she found that so appealing—or why she was suddenly looking forward to tonight so much.

Randall's voice boomed through the store pager. She'd been standing alone in the pharmacy aisle way too long, and he needed help. Seeing a few customers head toward the pharmacy department, she whirled around and ran smack-dab into Dee. Georgie staggered backward, rubbing her chest. However, the collision hadn't changed Dee's militant posture of folded arms and feet planted two feet apart.

"I can't believe it," Dee said with disgust.

"Wha—huh? Can't believe what?"

"That you've been holding out on me."

Georgie quickly hid her attack of guilt and thrust her chin up. "I don't have the foggiest idea what you're talking about." She brushed by Dee and continued her way back to the pharmacy.

"Georgie, if you saw what I just saw between you and Walt back there, you wouldn't be playing dumb with me right now," Dee charged from behind. "What's going on? I thought you said you and Walt were just friends."

Georgie stopped and slowly faced her friend. "I . . . Well . . . We are."

Dee gave her a mini eye roll. "Ugh. Believe me, there

wasn't an ounce of friendship in the way Walt just looked at you. Or the way you looked at Walt for that matter. Does Brad know?"

Georgie bristled at the mention of her brother. "Know what?"

"That his best friend and his only sister have the hots for one another." Dee began to laugh. "And it happened right under his nose. Actually, it's perfect if you really think about it. I'd like to see Brad interfere with *this* relationship."

"Relationship?" Her tongue stumbled over the word. "Oh, no. Walt and I may be attracted to one another—like you said—but it's nothing as serious as a relationship. And no, Brad doesn't know. He doesn't have to know. There's nothing to know. It's just . . . a little harmless dalliance."

Dee stared at her, skepticism pooling in her eyes. "What I just witnessed didn't look like a harmless dalliance. I hope you know what you're doing."

"Dee, don't worry. I'm a big girl. I know exactly what I'm doing."

"Do you?" she asked. "Then what exactly are you going to do about your date?"

"What date?"

"Your date with Clay Hayes."

Georgie's face fell and her eyes widened. She'd completely forgotten all about her celebrity date. It was coming up soon too. She had just filled out some more release forms a few days ago. She was so preoccupied with Walt, she hadn't even given it a second thought.

Dee shot her a smug grin. "Wonderful. I can see that you've got everything under control by the sheer panic-mode expression on your face." She took a step forward and lightly placed her hands on Georgie's shoulders. "Honey," she began, her voice low and sobering, "you better decide exactly what you want to do about Walt fast. Or else some-body could get hurt."

Georgie looked away and studied the ground. There was no use trying to convince herself—and Dee—that she only wanted friendship with Walt. The truth was she didn't want to go on that date with Clay Hayes. She didn't want to go out on *any* date with *anyone*. Except Walt. How had that hap-pened? She had convinced herself she could handle her at-traction to him and the inexplicable fear of losing control over her life if she had opened up her heart again. She thought she could keep Walt at arm's length. But now she had gone and completely fallen for him.

And she didn't know what she was going to do about it.

Chapter Twelve

The next night Georgie sat on the floor of her bedroom, looking through her family photo albums. It was the first time in a long time she'd even touched them. After her parents had died pictures had only magnified her loss, so she had avoided the reminders altogether. But she needed to see the photos now—really see them. A kind of therapy for the soul that was long overdue. Maybe if she finally faced her hurt, she wouldn't be so afraid to go through it again.

She turned the page and chuckled at the first picture she saw: her mother and father smiling down at a pimply-faced Brad holding an infant with orange fuzz on its head. Gosh, she was an ugly baby! But it was still a sweet picture. Brad looked stiff, almost as if he were afraid to drop or hurt her. Funny how his attitude toward her hadn't changed in all these years. Her brother still tried to protect her from harm.

Georgie flipped through to the next page and saw a picture of Walt and Brad posing in their high school football jerseys. She let out a little sigh at the memory. Would Walt hurt her? she wondered. Was it worth the risk of finding out? She wished her parents were here to offer her advice. She wanted to give in to her feelings for him, but what if Walt didn't really see her as someone more than Brad's little sister?

The sun had begun to set, but she was too emotionally drained to get up and turn on a light. It didn't matter. She was done looking at pictures, and the darkness fit her depressed mood.

A knock sounded at her door, and then Brad popped his head in. "What the—? Jeez, Georgie, what the heck's going on? What are you doing sitting in the dark like this?" he said, walking in and banging his toe against a box of photos.

"Praying for you to get a life, of course." With a smirk, she reached over and turned on the lamp by her night table.

"Oh, yeah? Thanks," he said with a cheesy grin. "While you're at it, you can pray I hit the lottery too."

"I'll see what I can do."

Brad motioned to the floor. "Hey, what's all this?" He bent down and started sifting through her box. "You're actually looking through our family photos?"

Georgie tried not to take offense at her brother's shocked tone. After all, she'd avoided these pictures for almost nine years. "Yeah. It's . . . I needed to."

Brad nodded as he started flipping through an album. The way he was intently gazing at the pages, she had a feeling he needed to see them again too. "Check this one out," he said, chuckling as he turned the album right side up for her to see.

Georgie's eyes welled with tears even though she was smiling. She'd forgotten her parents dressed up as Fred and Wilma Flintstone one year for Halloween. Her mother's face glowed with joy as her dad had struck a caveman pose for the camera. They looked so cute together. They had shared so much fun and love together. Something she'd taken for granted for as long as they were alive.

"They had a good marriage," she blurted.

Brad nodded, his eyes still on their parents' picture. "They had the best marriage."

Georgie closed the album and handed it back to him. "Do you want to get married someday?"

Brad's lips thinned. "No."

She blinked. She supposed she shouldn't be so surprised by his answer. What kind of man really went around hoping to get married anyway? But Brad was the sensitive type. Caring. Even if he hated to admit it, he would make a wonderful husband for some lucky woman. "You don't? Huh. Me either. That's kind of funny." Maybe they really were destined to be the only brother and sister spinster team in town.

Brad tossed the album back into the box with a decided *thump*, then folded his arm across his chest. "Oh, no it's not. That's not funny at all. You are definitely getting married. I don't want to hear you say something so crazy again."

"What? How come it's okay if you don't want to get married, but when I say it, I suddenly must be an escaped mental patient?"

Brad let out a laugh then ran his hands over and over through his hair until it stuck up in all directions. "You're not an escaped mental patient—at least, I don't think so." Georgie grabbed a pillow to throw at him, but he shot out his hand and blocked it.

"Look, Georgie," he said, his voice taking on a more serious tone, "it's not that I don't want to get married. I do . . . did. It's just that . . . I . . . I can't."

"Of course you can. It's not like it's against the law for . . ." Her mouth dropped open. She stared at her brother for several long seconds then jumped to her feet. "Oh, my gosh! You want to marry another man? Hey, that's okay.

Don't worry. If that's what you want, I think you can go to another state where it's legal and—"

"No, I don't want to marry another man," he said between clenched teeth. "Sheesh, Georgie. But it's so nice to know I'd have your full support if it were the case," he added dryly.

A bubble of laughter began to erupt inside of her, but she wisely cleared her throat to bank it down. "I don't understand. Why on earth can't you get married then?"

Brad didn't respond right away. He just closed his eyes and pinched the bridge of his nose, looking as if he'd rather be cleaning the toilet than having this discussion with her. "Because I can't marry someone who's already engaged to someone else."

"Well, duh, of course you can't. I know that." She began to mentally run down her knowledge of engaged women in town. Then a dawning of realization hit her between the eyes, and she covered her mouth in shock.

"Kendall," she whispered. "You're in love with Kendall, aren't you?"

Oh, my gosh. She should have seen the signs: the way he was so upset when Kendall announced her engagement, the way he never wanted to date, the way he even avoided Kendall and Jake's engagement party. What a dunce she was for not seeing it sooner. It all made sense.

Brad opened his eyes, and for the first time, she saw the raw pain he'd been so carefully hiding from her. "Oh, Brad," she said, shifting closer to him and taking his hands in hers. "I'm so sorry. Does Kendall know how you feel?"

He jerked his hands from hers. "No. And she's not going to find out," he said pointedly. "I should have told her how I felt earlier, but I didn't and now it's too late. I blew it and that's that. Now I just want to move on."

"But you're *not* moving on. Don't you see? You've been sitting around the house for months. I've been so worried about how you've been acting lately. I couldn't understand why you were so uninterested in dating. And now I learn it's all because of Kendall. Gosh, I even created a dating list for you."

Brad rolled his eyes. "Yeah, well, I want to move on, believe me. It's just . . . It's not easy. So back off for a little while longer. I promise when I'm ready you can give me that so-called list of yours, okay?" He stood, then held out his hands to help her up, giving her fingers a tight squeeze. "Look, Georgie, if I've been acting a little more overprotective than usual it's because I don't want you to waste your time like I did. I want you to find someone worthy of you. You deserve the best. I could have had the best with Kendall, but I was afraid. Don't be a coward like I was. Love is worth the risk."

Georgie blinked back tears. Worth the risk. Her brother didn't know it, but his pep talk was exactly what she needed to hear. Despite her fears, she knew now she should take that risk with Walt. She immediately jumped up and wrapped her arms around Brad, almost knocking the two of them over.

"Easy does it, kiddo," Brad said with a laugh. "You're not twelve anymore."

"Thanks for finally noticing," she said with a grin. "I was beginning to worry you and Walt weren't seeing me as an adult." Now she knew that wasn't true. She thought of the way Walt had treated her as an equal at the pharmacy, had looked at her, and had kissed her. Those were ways a man treated a woman. Not someone whom he saw as his friend's little sister.

Georgie reached up and planted a big sloppy kiss on his cheek. "You know what? You're the best brother in the whole world. Thank you."

"Uh, you're welcome," he murmured, swiping his cheek

with the back of his hand. "I think. Oh, by the way. Here." He reached into the back pocket of his jeans and held out a yellow envelope. "This just came in the mail today. I think that it's more stuff about that date contest."

She took the letter and stared at it. The thick paper felt like a bowling ball in her hand. She wondered if it was too late to get out of going on that date. She couldn't go. Not now. Not when she was in love with someone else. She wanted a relationship with Walt. Exclusively. A concept she didn't think she'd ever be able to embrace again.

Brad gestured to the letter. "Do you think the publicity from the contest is helping bring business in?"

She shook her head. "Not really. I think the diabetes expo we're having is doing more good. In fact, Walt's already talking about doing another health fair of some sort around Christmas. We're going to work on it together."

"So I guess there's no real reason you have to do this contest then, is there?"

"I—I suppose not."

Brad nodded solemnly. "Well, I want to keep the 'best brother in the whole world' title you've just bestowed upon me, so I won't say anything else on the subject." He stepped away and opened the door.

"Wait," she called.

She wanted to tell her brother about Walt, to share her feelings with him like he had with her, and to hear what he would think about her and Walt together. But when her brother turned around and gave her a questioning look, something held her back—she didn't know what—so she pasted on a smile instead. "Hey, thanks again."

The next day Georgie's heart pounded like a jackhammer as she slowly drove up to Walt's house. She could tell he was home. His truck was parked in the driveway, and she heard Pearl Jam's "Better Man" blaring through the windows. She chuckled, but as she let herself out of her car and walked up to the front door, she couldn't have agreed more with Eddie Vedder's lyrics. There wasn't a better man than Walt Somers. She could admit that now. *Let* herself admit that now and give in to the love she was once so afraid to face.

She juggled the gift she held in her arms and knocked on the door. Walt appeared in a matter of seconds, looking dusty, sweaty, and incredibly appealing in mesh navy shorts and a torn gray T-shirt that just said COLLEGE written across the chest in white block letters.

He opened the door and treated her to a magnificent smile that made her heart leap. "Well, well. You and Brad have another fight already?"

"Ha-ha," she said with a smirk, stepping into the house and gazing around at all the unopened boxes stacked around the living room. "Not at all. In fact, I can honestly say Brad and I have come to a complete understanding."

Walt shifted behind one of the boxes and turned down the music. "Too bad. I was hoping I was going to get a roommate," he said, with a wink.

His words unnerved her, and she almost dropped his gift. She thrust it in front of her before that happened. "Uh, here."

Walt's brows came together as he inspected the package. "What's this?"

"Just a little housewarming gift."

"Aw, you shouldn't have," he said with a grin.

"Well, maybe if you see what it is, you'll really mean those words."

With a chuckle, Walt placed it on top of the bar and began tearing at the blue wrapping. His eyes widened when he saw

what she gave him: a framed picture of the three of them—
Georgie, Walt, and Brad—on the beach as kids. Blown up
and in black and white. "This is great, Georgie!"

Georgie studied the picture in his hands. She came across
it when she had been looking through the old photos the
other night. The picture showed them all laughing in the wa-
ter playing with Georgie's father. Her mother must have
taken it when nobody had been looking. "You think so?" she
asked, hoping he meant it.

"Absolutely. I'm going to hang it right here in the foyer."

"I'm so glad you like it. I had forgotten how much my dad
had played with us. It was nice to . . . to think back on those
times again."

Walt put down the picture and gently took her hand and
kissed it. "Thanks to your family I did manage to have good
times, especially through my parents' divorce. Brad never
treated me differently when my mom left. And your parents,
well, they were the family I always wanted. I suppose that's
why I hung out at your house so much. When I was there,
everything seemed normal and perfect. This picture is a
great memory to have of that time in my life. Thank you."

She was so touched she didn't know what to say, which
was good because Walt didn't seem to be in a talkative
mood. He put his arms around her and lowered his head, first
kissing one corner of her mouth and then the other. She
melted immediately under the light touch of his lips and had
to wrap her arms around his waist to keep from falling over.
She could taste the toothpaste still on his tongue, feel the
desire radiating from his body. This was no simple "thank
you for the gift" kiss. Walt felt the same way she did about
him. And suddenly this risk she had chosen to take with him
didn't seem so risky at all.

"Knock, knock," came a cheery voice.

She and Walt broke apart, turning to see Kendall's bubbly smile beaming at them through the screen door. "Uh, I hope I'm not interrupting anything."

Georgie heard a small sigh escape Walt's lips as he walked over and opened the door for her. "Not at all. I was just, uh, thanking Georgie for her housewarming gift."

Kendall smirked. "Oh, well, I hope I get as nice a thank you, because I have a gift too." She held up a plate of banana muffins. "Fresh from the oven."

"Thanks." With a sheepish grin, Walt took the muffins from her. "Gee, I should have bought a house earlier. I've never had so many beautiful women come and bring me gifts."

Kendall laughed. "Keep telling me things I want to hear like that, and I'll be sure to visit more often." She cocked her head at Georgie. "I'm glad you're here. I was going to call you to see if you wanted to go to Singles' Night at O'Connell's Bar and Grill tonight."

"Singles' Night? But you're engaged." And for a brief moment—for Brad's sake—Georgie actually hoped Kendall was going to tell her she'd broken up with Jake.

"I know I'm engaged, silly," Kendall said with a laugh. "A few guys from one of the other platoons put a band together and are going to be playing there. Jake's platoon is on duty, and I didn't want to go alone."

Georgie quickly hid her disappointment. "Oh. Uh . . ."

Walt put down the muffins and cleared his throat. "You know I could use a break from all this unpacking. How about if I come too? That is, if you don't mind me hanging around."

Kendall's face brightened. "That's a great idea." Then she nudged Georgie with her elbow. "We don't mind Walt coming along with us at all, do we, Georgie?"

Georgie met Walt's gaze, and they shared a smile. "I don't mind at all."

Georgie was sure she was going to get stopped for speeding as she rushed home from work. Fortunately, she knew enough of the police force to talk her way out of a ticket but she didn't have any time to waste. She only had an hour before Walt picked her up tonight.

As soon as she got in the door, she dropped her purse and raced to her bedroom. She swung open her closet and was in the middle of surveying her pathetic lack of outfit choices when her brother walked in. Brad must have just gotten home from work himself since he was still in uniform.

"Hey, where are you headed to in such a hurry?" he asked, loosening the button of his work shirt collar.

"O'Connell's." She pulled out an apple-green halter top and held it out to him. "What do you think?"

"It's terrible."

She took a double-take at the shirt, then frowned. "It's not terrible. I ordered it from Talbots. And I happen to look fantastic in green." *And soon Walt will know how fantastic I look in it too.*

"No, not the top, Georgie. You going to O'Connell's is terrible. It's singles' night tonight, which means there will be a bunch of drunks, truckers, and unhappily married men perusing the female patrons. Sheesh, you already won that Clay Hayes date. Doesn't that fulfill your deadbeat quota for the month?"

She rolled her eyes. "Brad, you're doing it again. I thought you were going to take a break from this overprotective routine. Besides, I'm not going there to meet anyone. I'm going there to see a band with Kendall. And Walt," she added casually.

Brad's face washed with relief. "Oh, that's right. I forgot he'd be there with you."

Her insides twisted and she froze, the halter top still clenched in her fist. "What do you mean you forgot Walt would be there with me? You didn't even know I was going to O'Connell's with him until just now."

"Oh, uh . . ." Brad's face suddenly turned reddish-blue as if he were being choked—something she realized she was not far off from actually doing to him. He turned away and tried to slip out the door.

"Stop right there!" she shot before he could make a clean escape. Brad held up, teetering in the doorway with his back to her, one foot in her bedroom and the other foot in the hallway. "Brad, why did you say that? That you knew Walt would be with me. Did you talk to him earlier or something?"

"Not exactly." He slowly faced her, his apprehensive expression turning sheepish. He then gestured to the bed. "Listen, you better sit down."

Georgie tossed the halter top onto the bed and sat on it; she didn't worry about wrinkling it now. Brad's tone concerned her. His voice held the kind of seriousness she could see him using in his police job whenever he had to deliver bad news.

Brad gingerly sat down next to her, studying his hands for a moment before speaking. "Georgie, I've been worried about you lately."

"I know. I've been worried about you too. You seem—"

"Don't interrupt."

"Oh, sorry."

He gave her a withering look. "This is hard to tell you, but I think the whole Clay Hayes date thing made me nuts. Honestly, that's the only reason I would ever . . . I mean *I* couldn't so . . . Well, that's why I kind of asked Walt to kind of . . ."

Her throat tightened. "You kind of asked Walt to kind of what?"

"Keep tabs on you," he blurted.

Her mouth hung slightly open, and an intense sensation to break down swelled within her. Oh, my gosh, how stupid had she been? Brad had asked Walt for a favor, to keep an eye on her. Of course. No wonder Walt had been hanging around her so much. He didn't want to really be with her. He was just helping Brad keep an eye on his sister. Why had she thought Walt was any different?

"Oh, Brad, you big dumb idiot!" she cried, swatting him on the arm. "How could you do that to me?"

"I'm so sorry, Georgie. Walt was worried about you too. You know he loves you like a sister. I only asked him because I love you, and I didn't want any man taking advantage of you. I should have trusted your ability to take care of yourself more, but the whole Clay Hayes thing was the icing on the cake to what I'd been seeing in your life recently."

She swiped at a tear that had escaped her eye and looked at him. "What do you mean by what you've been seeing in my life recently?"

"Don't play dumb. You've been dating men that you—or any other woman for that matter—could never have a serious future with. I have eyes, Georgie. It's all about control with you. By hanging around all those losers you were guaranteeing yourself that you'd never fall in love."

Georgie closed her eyes, trying to absorb what Brad was saying, but only thinking about Walt and how betrayed she felt. He didn't see her as anything more than Brad's little sister after all. Those kisses they'd shared. Was it just a way to stick closer to her? Oh, gosh, she was going to be sick.

"I hope you can forgive me," Brad said.

Georgie opened her eyes and looked over at him, sitting

there with the sad soulful expression of a loyal basset hound. Despite her anger at him, she couldn't really blame him for being concerned. She *had* been avoiding relationships—and love. But with good reason. And this whole betrayal by Walt only affirmed why.

"Oh, Brad, you were right. Kendall told me the same thing, but I didn't want to admit it."

Brad nodded, then stood. "Look, why don't we talk about this later when we have time. You better get ready now."

"No, I'm not really in the mood to go out anymore." *Or face Walt.*

Brad lowered his gaze. "Sorry. Again, I didn't mean to ruin your night."

"I should call Kendall and tell her. Walt won't feel the need to go now that I'm not, and Kendall may not want to be there by herself."

"I'll go to O'Connell's with Kendall," Brad said.

"Are you sure?"

"Yeah," he said, looking anything *but* sure. "Look, I've been a lousy brother to you and a lousy friend to her. I might as well start making amends. Don't worry. Everything will be fine. I think I'm good. I mean I'm finally over her."

Georgie let out a wistful sigh. She could only hope she'd get over her feelings for Walt just as quickly.

Chapter Thirteen

W alt bounded up the steps of Brad and Georgie's condo, taking them two at a time, careful not to crush the bouquet of flowers he held. He wanted to do something special for Georgie, so on his way to pick her up he stopped by the florist. As soon as he saw the orange roses, they reminded him of her—warm as a sunset and sweet as citrus—and he had to get them. The clerk at the shop told him his choice symbolized passion and that giving a bouquet of orange roses denoted emerging romantic feelings and the desire to move a relationship beyond the stage of friendship.

Perfect.

Exactly what he wanted to convey to her. No more tiptoeing around the subject. He was in love with her, and he was going to tell her tonight.

Walt heaved a grateful sigh that Brad's car was not in the parking lot. He didn't want to have to explain the flowers—or his feelings—to his friend before he explained them to Georgie. He shifted the bouquet behind his back and rang the doorbell. When there was no answer, he rang the bell again.

Where was she? He checked his watch. Seven o'clock. He was right on time.

About to ring the bell again, he heard the deadbolt slide back, and then the door slowly swung open. Georgie stood in the doorway with her hair pulled up in a sloppy ponytail and her face devoid of makeup. Walt blinked as he eyed her up and down. Clad in a pink terrycloth robe and yellow slipper socks, Georgie hardly looked ready to go out. In fact, judging by the expression on her face, she hardly looked ready to let him inside.

"What are you doing here?" she asked, frowning up at him.

He wasn't sure what was going on, so he glanced behind to make sure she wasn't talking to somebody else. "What do you mean 'what am I doing here'? I thought we were going to O'Connell's."

Her gaze dropped to the hallway rug, and she shook her head. "I thought Brad called you. I'm not going to O'Connell's tonight. If you go now, you could probably still catch up with Brad and Kendall though." She stepped back and started to close the door.

"Wait." His hand shot out before she could shut it on him. What the heck was going on? She was so distant, so cold. He felt he was losing her before he even had her. "I'm not going to O'Connell's if you're not."

She snorted. "I figured as much."

"I'm not sure what you mean."

"Oh, Walt, just cut the dumb act, okay? Brad told me everything. You're a free man now. He doesn't want you spying and hanging around me anymore. And frankly, neither do I."

Brad had told her he wanted Walt to spy on her? Walt's insides turned cold as he realized what she must think of him. "Georgie, let me in. We need to discuss this. I can explain."

"There's no need. I understand perfectly. Brad asked for help in being a big brother to me, and you provided it just like the little loyal friend that you are. What's there to explain?"

"No, there's more. Let me in, and I'll tell you."

She hesitated, and for a moment he was sure she'd close the door in his face. But she stepped back grudgingly and allowed him to enter. He took the flowers out from behind his back and hurried in before she changed her mind.

"Nice touch," she said, pointing to the roses. "Were they supposed to play a part in your 'divert Georgie from her Clay Hayes date' operation?"

Walt ignored her barb. He walked over to the coffee table and gently placed the flowers down. Georgie clearly was hurt and wanted nothing more to do with him right now, but he had to remain calm or he'd ruin any hope of a future together. "No. There was no scheme. I just wanted you to have the roses, to show you how I feel." He took a deep breath. "I love you."

Georgie's face fell, and her shoulders stiffened. "Don't say that."

His heart raced as he took a step closer. He reached out and stroked her cheek, dipping his head so she could see his earnestness. "But it's true."

"No, it's not true." She backed away from him, lifting her chin, but not before he saw a flare of uncertainty in her eyes. "Otherwise, you wouldn't have agreed to spy on me."

"I wasn't spying. I . . ." He turned away and raked his hands through his hair in frustration. "Look, I only agreed to help Brad because you're naïve when it comes to men."

She let out a huff and folded her arms. "Yeah, that seems to be the mantra that I've been hearing around here lately. Well, you'll be happy to learn—as I've already informed Brad—I can take care of myself. Thanks for the brotherly concern, though."

"My concern isn't brotherly, Georgie. I love you. What more do I have to do or say?"

"I think you've done enough." She walked over to the door and swung it open, indicating for him to leave. "Love isn't about controlling a person's life."

"I wasn't trying to control your life. You're being irrational. If you'd just—"

"If I'd just what? Let you and Brad keep me in a cocoon for the rest of my life? No thank you. I think you better go."

Silence fell between them as he stood in the middle of the room. His gaze burned into hers, praying she'd wake up and see his point of view, but she quickly broke eye contact.

So this was it? No further discussion? She was just going to push him away like an unwanted trespasser. He couldn't believe what was happening. She obviously didn't realize he wouldn't let her go so easily. Nothing was going to stop him from convincing her that they were meant to be together. For now he'd have to bide his time until she was in a better frame of mind.

Walt dragged himself toward the door. As soon he stepped into the hallway, he turned around and couldn't resist trying one last time. "You know, Georgie, when a person cares about another person, they do things to protect them—sometimes crazy things. Act crazy. Love does that to people. I just didn't want to see you get hurt."

She gazed up at him, her eyes conveying a mixture of sadness and tears. "Yeah. Well, I'm afraid you're too late for that." Then she closed the door with a decided click.

Walt came home from work with a headache. Business at the pharmacy was picking up, there was still some last minute finalizing to be done on the diabetes expo, and they were short on help since Georgie decided to use up her vacation days. No doubt, she was avoiding him. She didn't even want to call and speak to him. Instead, she went over his head and got approval to take time off from Al. Now not only their personal relationship was suffering, but their working relationship as well. He had screwed things up royally.

Walt hadn't seen or spoken to Brad in a while either. Had Georgie mentioned anything to him about their fight? It seemed as if everything in Walt's personal life was falling apart. Thank goodness business was doing well at least. He and his uncle would be able to hold on to the pharmacy for a while if things continued like they had been. He could keep his house and stay in town. But he needed to get Georgie back in his life, or it would all mean nothing.

Walt rubbed his temples, trying to decide what the next best plan of action would be with Georgie when he heard knocking. He looked up and frowned when he saw Brad through the screen door. Even though Walt hadn't seen him in a while, something in his friend's expression and stance had Walt thinking Brad was not here simply for a relaxed social visit.

He walked over and opened the storm door. "Hey, what brings you by?" he asked, trying to keep his voice casual.

"Georgie."

A crushing sensation formed in Walt's chest—part guilt, part frustration, part misery. He must have hurt her pretty badly for her to confide everything to her brother. Obviously Brad hated him now too.

"Clay Hayes and his entourage just picked her up," Brad continued. He sighed, then looked around the room with tired eyes. "You have anything to drink around here? I could use a cold beer."

Walt blinked. "Wait. What do you mean Clay Hayes and

his entourage just picked her up? The Clay Hayes date is to-night?"

Brad looked at him with surprise. "Yeah. It was in all the papers this week. Where have you been?"

Where *had* he been?

Drowning his sorrows by throwing all his time and energy into the pharmacy. Walt had heard Dee and some customers discussing the upcoming celebrity date, but he had tuned their conversations out. He was too preoccupied with the business, missing Georgie, and feeling sorry for himself to care.

Brad shook his head in disgust. "You should have seen what Georgie was wearing. That creep Clay Hayes looked as if he hit the jackpot when saw her standing there in those black knee-high boots of hers. If his bodyguard wasn't in the way, I would've decked him one right in that pointy chin of his."

Georgie in knee-high boots? Walt closed his eyes and tried to block out that sexy image.

And failed.

"Oh, hell," he murmured.

Brad nodded. "I know what you mean. But the guys han-dling Clay Hayes' police escort told me for security reasons their date won't be too private, so that's one less thing to worry about. Plus, Georgie is a lot tougher than I thought. You were right about that. It just drives me crazy that she's wasting her time with this whole escapade, you know?"

Yeah. Walt knew. It was driving him crazy too. Mostly, because Georgie should be here wearing those knee-high boots for him and not for some soap star hack. But the whole situation was so typically Georgie. She went on that date to spite Walt. She obviously had strong feelings for him or it wouldn't matter so much to try to hurt him like this. Only, Walt didn't care about the date. He didn't care what she did, just as long as she would forgive him and love him back. Why couldn't she let go and admit her feelings? He wearily sat on his sofa and put his head in his hands, wishing he wasn't in love with such a stubborn woman.

Brad walked over and plopped down next to him. "Hey, it looks as though you could use a stiff drink too. How about I go home, change, and meet you at O'Connell's? That'll cheer us up."

"No, I don't think so," he mumbled.

"Why not?"

Walt heaved a frustrated sigh. There was no use in worrying what his friend thought anymore. It was time to be honest about his feelings and tell Brad the truth. "I love your sister," he said through his hands.

"Yeah, me too. But don't worry. Georgie will be fine tonight."

Walt popped his head up. "No. I mean I love her."

"I know," Brad said sympathetically. "Me too. Now let's go—"

Walt raised a hand to cut him off. "No, Brad. You don't understand. I don't just love her. I'm *in* love with her."

Brad looked as if he were about to say something but then his expression went blank, and he went very still. "Wait," he said, blinking. "What did you say? You mean . . . ?"

Walt nodded grimly.

Brad sat back with a loud *whoosh,* and for several long minutes he stared off into space, his mouth hung slightly open, as if the hard drive in his brain suddenly crashed. Not quite the reaction Walt had wished for when he finally decided to break the news, but all in all Brad was taking the announcement better than expected.

Brad shook his head, then finally refocused on Walt. He leaned in and grabbed a fistful of Walt's T-shirt. "Listen, you better be straight with me. Are you telling me you love my sister as in . . . until death do us part?"

Walt eased back, gingerly trying to pry out the few chest hairs Brad had managed to capture when he grabbed his shirt. "Yeah, I'm not kidding."

"I'm not sure how I feel about this. I mean, you're like a brother to her."

Walt shook his head. "No, Brad. *You're* her brother. I didn't mean to fall in love with your sister. But I've never loved anyone like I love her."

"You and Georgie, huh?" Several beats went by, then a slow smile spread across Brad's mouth. He finally let go of Walt's shirt and slapped him on the back. "Well, all right then, So what are you doing here? She needs to know this. Go barge in on Georgie's date with Mr. Not So Wonderful and tell him to get his own woman."

"I can't barge in on her date. That would ruin everything. Besides, I tried to tell her how I feel, but she's too mad at me to listen. It was her choice to go on that date. Now I have to step back for a while. She doesn't want any more interference in her life. Thanks to you, I think I've done enough of that."

"Oh, I'm sorry, man. I didn't think she'd be mad at you too."

"It's all right. You didn't know how I felt about her. I should have told you and her earlier anyway, but I was afraid to face those feelings myself."

Brad nodded once and stood. "Listen, forget about O'Connell's. I'm going to head home now and wait for Georgie to get back from her date." He walked over to the front door and let himself out. "One more thing, Walt," he said through the screen. "You may not believe me, but I'm not going to interfere in your love life even though it does happen to involve my only sister. Just . . . don't hurt her. Or I *will* hurt you."

Walt let out a little smile. "Believe me, I know what I'm getting into."

"Well, thanks for being upfront with me—and her."

"Yeah, a lot of good it's done me. She won't even talk to me now."

Brad shrugged and dropped his gaze. "It's better to take that gamble with love and lose than to not gamble at all," he said sadly.

As Brad walked away, Walt had a funny feeling that his friend had some experience behind that cliché he offered. Unfortunately, Brad's encouraging words still didn't make him feel any better.

"One more picture!" someone shouted.

In response, Clay Hayes wrapped his arm around Georgie's waist, bringing her in close—*too* close, in her opinion, considering she'd soon have an imprint of his belt buckle on her pelvis—and flashed a brilliant smile for the camera. Two more flashes went off, then the owner of the restaurant stepped outside and announced their table was ready. The cameramen groaned, but they started to pack up their equipment, since they weren't allowed in the dining area.

Clay Hayes gazed down at her and tightened his arms around her, unknowingly sending his belt buckle deeper into her skin. "Are you hungry?" he murmured.

Hungry? He had to be kidding. Her thoughts were hardly on food. Becoming impaled in the middle of the sidewalk was at the forefront of her mind.

"Starving!" she cried and shoved him away, hoping to prove her point, and perhaps stop any further bleeding. She quickly looked at her middle. Thank goodness everything was still intact.

Clay smiled down at her. Whether it was because he found her enormous appetite amusing or he was just being polite, she couldn't be sure. He did seem like a nice guy, though, even better looking in person than on TV, and hardly the kind of womanizer Brad and Walt had portrayed him to be. Not that he was Mr. Personality. She quickly found out Clay—and his publicist—didn't have much of a sense of humor, especially when Brad proceeded to grill them on what he had in mind for their date tonight.

Clay took hold of her free hand and led her inside the restaurant. Since she was more familiar with the town, Clay let her choose where they would eat. She chose the Purple Grape, a restaurant known for its trendy ambiance and winery, mostly because it was a favorite with the locals. She figured if the conversation between her and Clay ever lagged, she'd see someone she knew and be able to strike up more chitchat.

As she followed Clay, she was comforted to see a few familiar faces from the pharmacy. They waved, and she happily waved back. Clay, on the other hand, kept his chin down and gaze focused on the hostess leading the way to their table. His lighthearted mood seemed to come and go with the camera, and she couldn't help but wonder what she'd gotten herself into.

They were shown a nice quiet table in the corner of the restaurant, made even more private by several potted trees. Georgie sat down and opened up her menu, mentally kicking herself when her gaze went right for the dessert column. She saw *white chocolate cheesecake* and was reminded of when she and Walt had shared a piece the last time they'd been out together. Walt had called that night a special occasion since it was the first time they had been in each other's company without fighting. But that night had been special for another reason; it was the first time Walt had kissed her.

No, no. Stop it! You're out on a date with Clay Hayes for goodness sakes, and you're thinking about another man? Are you an idiot or something?

Apparently she was. Because here she was on a perfectly nice—although not as exciting as she'd thought—date with Hollywood heartthrob Clay Hayes, and all she could think about was how she wished she were on a date with Walt. She missed him. His laugh, his smile, even the overboard concern he had for her well-being. She'd thought she'd done the right thing by avoiding him this past week, but not seeing him only made her think about him even more.

Why wasn't he here? Brad probably had told him by now that she'd left on her date. She half expected Walt to do something crazy when he found out, like barge in on her date and demand she come home with him. Only . . . Walt wasn't barging through the doors. He obviously had listened to her when she'd said she could take care of herself and make her own decisions. Which was good. For the best, really. But . . .

This was so unlike Walt. Didn't he care about her anymore?

Clay snapped his fingers in front of her to get her attention. It did, but the rudeness of it also didn't win him any points with her. "Why do you keep staring at the doors?" he asked. "Aren't you having a good time?"

"No, no, I'm having a great time," she said, pasting on a smile and willing her gaze to focus on Clay's nose and not the front door of the restaurant. "It's just that . . ."

Clay put down his menu, giving her his full attention. "Are you expecting someone?"

Georgie blinked. He was a more perceptive person than

she thought or even gave him credit for, and suddenly she felt guilty for allowing herself to be so transparent. "Well . . ."

"I won't tell you I'm surprised. You're a beautiful woman, Georgiana."

She blushed, then smiled a little at his use of her full name. For as long as she could remember, people in town who knew and loved her had only called her Georgie. Including Walt. "Thank you."

"I'm a little disappointed that I couldn't make you forget about another man. I've been doing these date contests all over the country. You're the first woman I've met who's had both beauty and brains."

Walt had said the exact same thing about her. Her gaze dropped to her lap when she realized how foolish she'd been about misjudging Walt's feelings about her. Walt had said he loved her too. But she had been afraid of her feelings, of becoming so attached to him, and she had used her anger at him as an excuse to push him away.

"This is also the first contest I've done where I've had someone spy on me from behind a fake tree," he added.

Georgie's gaze snapped up. "What? Someone's spying?" Her heart lifted. She wanted to turn around and look, but didn't want the perpetrator to realize he'd been pointed out so soon.

Walt. It had to be Walt. He had come to spy on her date. She knew it! Half of her was overjoyed—and the other half infuriated.

Oh, gosh. Did love always make you feel so mixed up?

"Don't worry," Clay said. "I'll handle it." He signaled for his bodyguard to approach the table.

"No. Wait," she said, laying a hand on his arm. "I'll handle it."

An eyebrow arched up. "Oh? Get this a lot, do you?"

She rolled her eyes. "Let's just put it this way. The past few weeks have made me a pro." Not that she was complaining anymore.

Clay was shaking his head in amusement as she stood from the table. Her gaze darted around the room, then she walked toward the tree whose leaves had begun to shake.

Could he be more obvious? Walt's spying techniques were pathetic. But it didn't matter. She was just so glad to have him concerned about her again. She couldn't wait to tell him just that, and she doubled her steps. When she reached the tree, she quickly parted the branches to catch him by surprise. "Ah-ha!" she cried.

Dee and Kendall's shocked faces stared back at her.

Chapter Fourteen

Kendall grabbed her chest and sprang up from her kneeling position. "Good heavens, Georgie!" She visibly swallowed, then tried to catch her breath. "What on earth would make you sneak up and scare us like that?"

Georgie ignored the question and quickly scanned the dining area instead. *Where was Walt?* There was no sign of him anywhere. Huh. So he hadn't come for her after all. She fingered her bottom lip and looked around one more time.

Walt definitely wasn't there.

She didn't know how to feel about his absence. This was what she wanted after all, to be left to her own decisions, to not have him or Brad interfere with her life. Apparently Walt finally got the message. But something suddenly didn't feel right about it. Did she actually miss his overprotecting now? She certainly wasn't feeling smothered any longer. But she wasn't exactly feeling loved any longer either. There were just so many times a man would take being pushed away.

What had she done?

"Are you all right?" Dee asked, breaking into her thoughts.

Hardly. In fact, her chest hurt and she was about to burst into tears.

"I . . . I think so," Georgie lied, rubbing her heart. She looked at them and the overly concerned expression on her friends' faces snapped her back to the matter at hand. "Hey, you guys have a lot of nerve being mad at me for scaring you. Just what do you think you're doing playing *Alias* with a plastic birch tree? Clay Hayes could have you both arrested."

"Arrested?" Kendall squeaked. "He wouldn't!"

No, Clay Hayes probably wouldn't. He seemed too nice a guy. But Dee and Kendall didn't know that. "What are you guys doing here anyway? Did Brad or Walt send you to check up on me?" she asked, not sure what she was hoping to hear.

Dee and Kendall exchanged guilty looks. "No," Dee finally said. "We're here because we were worried about you."

"Good heavens," Georgie mumbled as she slapped a hand over her forehead. "Please tell me you didn't just say what I think you said." Her friends were worried about her. Wonderful. First Brad, then Walt, and now them. If this wasn't the end-all kicker in the pants to this last month's overprotective craze, she didn't know what was.

Kendall's gaze flickered with a brief flash of uneasiness toward where Clay Hayes was sitting. She licked her lips before she spoke. "Georgie, Dee and I have a confession to make."

Georgie's mouth fell open. "Oh, no," she groaned. No! No more confessions! She wasn't sure how many more admissions her heart could take in a week.

"You know how you were wondering how you won this date?" Dee asked. "I mean since you hadn't entered yourself in the contest? Well, surprise. Kendall and I entered you. But you were harping on a lot about Brad ruining all your dates," she rushed on to explain, "so we thought it would be almost impossible to ruin a highly publicized one."

Georgie closed her eyes, thinking about how all those foolish things she'd been doing lately must be catching. "So you thought it'd be better if you guys ruined my date instead of Brad?"

Kendall chuckled. "No, of course not. We didn't mean to mess your date up, but after all that stuff Brad said about Clay Hayes . . . well, we thought we made a mistake and just wanted to make sure you were okay. And since Walt—"

"What about Walt?" Georgie interrupted. Her gaze darted to the door again. "Is he outside?"

"Uh, well, no. We stopped by his house on the way here, because we figured he'd want to come with us. But he was determined not to come here and interfere."

"Oh. Right." Georgie's heart sank. "That's . . . good. I mean I did accuse him of trying to control my life." Funny, but now that Walt was out of her life, her life felt more out of control than ever.

"But weren't you sort of trying to control Brad's life?" Dee gently pointed out.

"No, I—" Georgie's eyes widened. Yes, she had been interfering with her brother's love life. But it was different. It was because . . . She blinked several times. Because she loved her brother, she had been trying to interfere in his love life and find him a woman. Oh, great. She had been doing exactly what she accused Brad and Walt of doing in her life. There wasn't any difference at all. Tears formed in her eyes at the thought of how foolish she'd acted toward them. "Somebody please shoot me," she said in defeat. "I think I may have ruined things with Walt over my stupidity."

"Honey, Walt told us about your fight," Kendall said. "He sure looked miserable, didn't he, Dee? Like it was taking all the willpower in the universe not to think about you out with another man."

Georgie dabbed at her eyes. "You really think so?"

Kendall nodded emphatically. "Walt loves you, honey. I think that's why he's not here. He's trying to give you what you said you wanted. No pressure. No interference. You *do* still want that, right?"

Did she? Georgie thought her legs were about to give way. Dee must have thought so too, because she grabbed a chair and slid it under her. Walt still loved her. And he was trying to show her that. Only she didn't want him butting out of her life anymore. She wanted him *in* her life. She loved Walt's overprotectiveness. She loved Walt.

Was it too late to tell him all that?

She looked up at her friends. They loved her too, and because of that, decided to spy on her date with a famous actor. She almost laughed out loud. Was this the crazy stuff you did for people you care about that Walt had tried to explain to her? If so, she had been a fool for not realizing this sooner. And she decided she was about due to start doing some crazy stuff herself.

"I'm going to find Walt," she announced, feeling stronger and hopeful at just saying the words.

Her friends' faces lit up like Fourth of July fireworks. "Thank goodness!" Dee exclaimed. "I thought you'd never come to your senses and make up with him."

Kendall grabbed her arm as Georgie stood. "Yeah, we're both happy for you and that's great and all, but what about, uh, you know who?"

Georgie frowned. "Who?"

"Clay Hayes," Kendall said, motioning behind her.

Georgie glanced over her shoulder at Clay, who appeared

to be happy enough flirting with one of the waitresses. "Oh, he'll understand," she said with a smirk. "I have a feeling Clay was just looking for a fling anyway."

Walt tapped his pencil against the kitchen table as he pored over the pharmacy's business reports. He figured the best way to forget about Georgie's date with a handsome TV personality—who had little regard for unassuming beautiful women—was to peruse through two months' worth of profit and loss statements. He already noticed the pre-scription count had gone up by over a thousand for the month.

See? He was totally focused on work and not on Georgie. In fact, he was able to completely block out all the smarmy lines Clay Hayes could be using on her tonight. Hadn't thought twice about how incredible Clay Hayes must be finding the scent of Georgie's hair right now. And he definitely forgot all about those black boots she was wearing now too.

That did it. He shot up out of his seat and his pencil and papers flew to the floor. Who was he kidding? There was only one way to end his maddening thoughts of Georgie. He was going to have to barge in on her "good time" with Mr. Movie Star and make sure she was all right.

He marched over to the TV and started flipping channels. There had to be some news report on their date and where they were headed tonight. Then he found it. *Entertainment Tonight* said the couple was having a wonderful time so far and had plans to have dinner at a trendy new restaurant in the shore town.

Trendy? Here in Maritime City? He scratched his head. He could think of maybe two possible restaurants. There wasn't time to waste if he had to check them both out. He grabbed his jacket, flung the door open, and crashed right into a warm body. A soft, warm body who squeaked and smelled like . . . Georgie.

"Georgie?" He reached out with both hands to steady her— and himself. His mind had trouble focusing. He couldn't believe Georgie was actually standing in front of him. She looked liked an angel—in knee-high biker boots. Those boots looked even better in real life than in his imagination. He gazed into her eyes and was filled with so many emotions, so many things he wanted to say to her, he didn't know where to start. "I like your shoes," he said.

I like your shoes?

After spending a torturous week apart that's the first thing he says to her?

The corners of Georgie's mouth quirked up. "Thanks. I like yours too."

Walt looked down and realized he was barefooted. In his haste to find Georgie and rip her out of Clay Hayes' arms he had forgotten his shoes.

"Um, were you going somewhere?" she asked.

"Yeah." *To find you.* But here she was. His hands automatically tightened on her shoulders. He had her now, and he wasn't about to let go anytime soon. "Why aren't you on your date now? Did Clay Hayes try anything?"

Her chin lifted. "Would you have cared if he had?"

"Georgie, stop playing these games," he snapped as he searched her face for the truth. "Why are you here? Are you hurt?"

She looked down and nodded solemnly.

"Son of a—" He sprung back, rage eating at his insides. He grabbed her hand and began pulling her down the steps. "We'll call Brad on the way. Right now we're going to go pay Clay Hayes a visit. He better have the number of a good plastic surgeon, or his TV days will be over."

"No, stop," she said, digging in her heels and yanking him to a stop. "Wait."

"What do mean wait? If that guy hurt you, he needs to answer for it."

Georgie shook her head, her eyes brimming with sadness. "He wasn't the one who hurt me, Walt. You were."

Walt closed his eyes and took a deep breath. His nerves were wound up tightly over what he'd thought Clay Hayes had done to her. But she was okay. Thank God. Physically at least. Emotionally she was still hurt. And it was his own fault.

"Walt, I need to know something. Were you really not going to interfere with my date with Clay Hayes?"

He opened his eyes and gazed down at her beautiful face. He really wished he had the answer she wanted to hear, but he couldn't help the way he was. Whether she wanted him to or not, whether she loved him or not, he would always look out for her best interests. There was no changing that. "To be honest, I *was* going to interfere. I tried to stay away, but the thought of you two together was driving me nuts. In fact, I was on my way over to find you before you showed up on my doorstep. I know this news isn't going to make you happy. I'm sorry, but—"

Georgie flung herself into his arms right then, her mouth landing squarely on his. He staggered back a few steps. But his shock passed quickly, and his arms came around her, bringing her in close. He wanted this so badly and thought he'd never have the opportunity again. She felt so warm, tasted so good. He'd missed the feel of her body and the scent of her hair. He'd missed *her* and almost melted in relief at having her in his arms again. But he needed to make sure she was in his arms for the right reasons.

"Georgie," he said against her lips.

"Hmm?" She tilted her head back ever so lightly, a mild glint of amusement in her eyes.

"Not that I'm complaining, but maybe you didn't understand what I was telling you. I was purposely going to try to break up your evening with Clay Hayes tonight."

A small smile broke out on her lips. "I know."

"You know? And you're okay with that?"

"I'm more than okay with it. In fact, when you hadn't shown up at the restaurant, I actually missed you not looking after me. I realized—even after all my complaining about having people interfere with my life—I was guilty of doing the same thing to Brad. You were right. Love does make you do crazy stuff." She looked down at his feet again with a smug smile. "Maybe even things like rush out of a house without shoes to protect the woman you love?"

"Yes, that's right, because I do love you." He grinned and was about to bring his lips down to hers again when he heard her murmur, "I love you too." At that moment there wasn't much—aside from a house fire—that would get him to stop kissing Georgie, but those four words did the trick. He backed away a little and took in the dazzling woman standing in front of him, the woman he loved more than anything in the world.

The woman who just said she loved him back.

"Just so you know," he told her teasingly, "love me, love my protective nature. You better get used to it. I'm always going to love you and look out for you, Georgie, for as long as we both shall live."

She sighed a contented sigh, as she cupped his face. "I'm counting on it. Just as long as *you* know, I'll be loving you back and looking out for *you* always too, for as long as we both shall live."

"I'm making you put that in our wedding vows."

She laughed. "Deal."

"But, ah, just promise me one more thing."

Her brow wrinkled. "What's that?"

"Don't enter any more contests."

"Okay, I promise," she said, planting another kiss on his lips. "Besides, who needs to enter any contests when I already have the best prize around?"

"I'm glad you think that." He grinned and wrapped his arms around her tighter. "Otherwise I'd have to sic your brother on you."